MW01076798

COLD SILENCE - A CHRISTIAN ROMANTIC SUSPENSE

A COLD HARBOR NOVEL - PREQUEL

SUSAN SLEEMAN

EDGE OF YOUR SEAT BOOKS, INC.

Published by Edge of Your Seat Books, Inc.

Contact the publisher at contact@edgeofyourseatbooks.com

1

Captain Travis Chapman readily served wherever his country needed him. All Green Berets did.

But this?

"I realize this operation is a bit unusual." Colonel Louis Vogler grabbed a marker and approached the whiteboard in the small Fort Bragg briefing room.

Unusual? Try earthshaking.

Travis tugged at his collar and swallowed the unease threatening to bring up his breakfast. He had to find a way out of this assignment. For once, he didn't care what the team needed. This was personal. He'd do anything else. Go anywhere other than the Army Research Institute in Orlando.

Getting quickly and quietly behind enemy lines and creating insurgencies was what he knew and thrived on—it was how he lived and operated day to day. But working with Claire at the institute? With the woman who'd left him feeling as if a grenade had exploded in his chest, his heart still a torn mess two years later?

Not that.

He shifted in his chair and watched the colonel ink

Combat Action and Tactics Simulator on the board in bold red strokes. Vogler turned, dark brows thick as caterpillars drawn together, perpetual scowl fixed on his broad face. "As I mentioned, your familiarity with CATS makes you the ideal candidate for this op."

CATS. Claire's pet project to develop a lower-cost alternative to the Army's current simulated training program. Travis had spent months by her side working out kinks in it. Discussing enhancements for the prototype. Getting to know her and...

Not going there again.

"Is there a problem with this assignment, Captain?" Vogler's penetrating gaze raked over him.

Travis sat up straighter and dug his nails into his palms, pain biting into his skin and keeping him on task. "No, sir, but with all due respect, are you sure this op is appropriate for our team?"

The crease between Vogler's brows deepened, but his eyes remained riveted on Travis. "Didn't mention the team. They're spinning up tonight as planned. This will be just you and your qualifications. You know the facility and CATS."

And Claire.

Even now, with Vogler watching him intently, Travis could get lost in thoughts of her. The smell of her perfume with a hint of lavender in direct contrast to her down-to-earth personality, almost lingered in the air. He could see her sparkling eyes behind designer glasses. What would've happened if she hadn't rejected him?

Stop it. You've asked that like a thousand times. No point in it. None.

Vogler shifted on the balls of his feet, impatience written on his face. "Is there something you need to tell me, Captain?"

I once believed in a forever kind of love and, thanks to Claire, now I don't. Yeah, right. Like he'd tell Vogler that.

"No, sir. I just need the op details to catch my flight on time." He opened the briefing folder, the op dubbed Operation Cold Silence, but he had no idea why the title. "So are they looking for me to participate in testing and give the simulator a Green Beret seal of approval?"

"Negative. It's more involved than that. Project director Dr. Claire Reed has completed a solid prototype. A copy of the software and a virtual device were stolen from the institute last night. Preliminary investigations by Reed point to an inside job, though I must say she's having a hard time believing anyone on her team could do this."

At Vogler's use of Claire's name, Travis's brain snapped to full attention. "Why an inside job?"

Vogler raised his index finger. "First, stealing the software is worthless without the ability to overcome the encryption and obfuscation techniques employed as security features. Only an insider would have that information."

"That information could've been stolen too."

"True, but less likely, and our other factors point to an insider."

"Factors such as?"

"Few people outside the staff would know the value of Reed's breakthrough. She's taken a technology that has cost us billions of dollars and made it affordable. Means if it was available on the black market, even small guerrilla groups would have the money to turn our training against us."

Travis shuddered at the thought of the many insurgent groups he'd trained over the years and imagined similar groups whose values opposed America's using the U.S. Army's exacting standards to train an unlimited number of soldiers.

"Exactly." Vogler rested on the edge of the table and

lifted another finger. "Also, the thief would have to get past the guards to get on campus."

"Not an impossible task, but difficult," Travis said as he remembered the guard post at the campus front gate. "I doubt the thief waltzed through the front gate, but can you get the log book and security feed for last night?"

"Can do, but I think you're wasting your time," Vogler said. "There's no sign of a break-in, and the only sign of the theft—other than the missing equipment and download of the software—was a problem with security cameras. They were either disabled or malfunctioned last night around 2300 hours for about an hour, but the institute's exits showed no sign of forced breaching, and the alarm wasn't activated."

Travis ran through what he remembered from his prior time on site. "Employees access the institute by key card during operating hours. Key cards are tied to each employee, and we can identify who came and went and at what time. This is true for everyone. Only exception is the time for management who have extended hours. But when I worked there, it was cut off at 2200 hours and needed special permission from Dr. Reed to be on site after that."

"Nothing has changed." He narrowed his gaze. "There was no key card access last night. If there had been, it would point to an individual and there would be no need for your services."

Curiouser and curiouser. "How did the thief get in?"

"That's one of the big questions we need to answer, and why I called you in."

Surely they didn't think his skills were needed here. His deployments on ops usually took him to sub-Saharan Africa in covert operations, not hunting down a thief in the United States. "Won't local investigators handle this breach?"

Vogler shook his head. "We aren't informing law

4

enforcement of the theft. This requires covert skills to keep the investigation under wraps. Plus, in addition to locating the thief, you'll provide protection for Reed."

"Cl—Dr. Reed—needs protection?" The words shot out of Travis's mouth before he could filter them.

Vogler eyed him for a long moment before replying. "We believe she's at risk for abduction, and we need to put our strongest man in place to keep her out of enemy hands."

Questions swirled in Travis's brain, mixing with concern for Claire. "I don't understand. If the thief got what he was after, why would she be in danger?"

Vogler's jaw firmed. Travis knew his commanding officer well enough to know he wouldn't like the next words out of his mouth. He braced himself.

"Because of the simulator's value, the project team opted to keep certain details out of the written specifications," Vogler said, pausing to flex the muscles in his jaw. "That way, if the technology ever fell into the wrong hands, the prototype would be useless without this additional information. Of course, the data is on file at a secured location, but other than that, Reed is the only person who possesses the information. Security at the offsite facility makes stealing the written documentation impossible so—"

"The only way the thief can deploy the prototype is by obtaining the specs from Dr. Reed," Travis finished as a sense of foreboding settled over him. "Which means if this really is an inside job, then the thief knows she alone holds the key and will likely force her to share it."

"Hence her need for protection."

Travis had way too much experience in obtaining information from noncompliant subjects, and he couldn't abide thoughts of Claire in such a situation.

And maybe being killed once she provided the information and they no longer needed her.

The room closed in on him. He dug at the knot on his tie. He wanted to help Claire, really he did, but could he let go of his personal feelings long enough to achieve this goal on his own? "Seems to me deploying the entire team would be more effective than sending one guy."

Vogler shook his head hard, the steely resolve he was known for lifted his shoulders even higher than his already near-perfect posture. "A team of twelve would alert the institute staff to the problem. No one but Reed and her superiors at the institute know about the theft. We want to keep it that way. We don't want to send the thief into hiding or force him to act immediately on abducting Reed. You'll go in under the guise of testing the latest equipment. That allows you to stay close to Reed and quietly investigate while no one is the wiser on the theft."

Stay close to Reed. Close to Claire. A distraction that could threaten his performance.

"I have also requested civilian support from a world-class forensic lab—the Veritas Center. I'm told they're the best of the best not only in physical crime forensics but IT as well. And as a bonus, they're out of Portland, Oregon, so if one of them lets it slip about the case, which I highly doubt, it shouldn't make it back to Orlando."

Operation Cold Silence. The op name was starting to make sense. Claire had to remain silent on the code and everyone investigating had to keep it quiet too.

"They're sending a team to process the facility after hours tomorrow," Vogler continued. "I'll expect you to coordinate with their team leader and report on the crime scene findings." He handed Travis a packet of papers. "We have a flight that will put you on the ground for business opening in the morning."

"Yes, sir," Travis said, trying to sound enthusiastic about

his assignment, though he had no experience with crime scenes.

"You can handle this, Chapman." Vogler crossed his arms, his shoulders remaining in a hard line, proving he didn't intend to back down. "You've gathered intelligence on enemies before and have plenty of experience in capturing high-value targets. Simply consider this thief high-value and you'll succeed."

"That I can do."

"I'll text you the contact details for the Veritas Center's forensic expert. After they complete their evaluation and you do your initial assessment of the situation, I'll entertain requests for deploying additional support. But keep in mind that this operation remains on the QT until I say otherwise."

Fine. Travis got it. A covert mission it would be. A forensic team for one night then basically him and Claire alone. The last thing he wanted, but he would do it. And do it well. "You can count on me, sir."

"We always do," Vogler said, then dismissed Travis.

In the hallway, Travis glanced at the flight details from the colonel and his watch. He had barely enough time to check a handgun out of the armory and pack his duffle then take a quick flight from North Carolina to Orlando. He would touchdown that night and be at Claire's side first thing in the morning, as Vogler had said. That gave him a short time to work through residual issues with Claire and get his head in the game.

Failure to clear his brain could put her right in the enemy's hands—costing Claire her life.

Claire Reed's dream had been stolen. Right here, in the dark of night in her home away from home. She glanced at the sign on the exterior of the tall building. Bold black letters mounted on stucco painted a cheery yellow read: *Army Research Institute.*

Her sanctuary. Until yesterday morning when she'd discovered the theft.

She settled her foot on a concrete planter filled with swaying grasses and gently stretched her tight leg muscles. Music pelted from the outdoor speaker, a pop song referencing shades of winter.

Winter, right. Not in this eighty-degree temperature even at seven a.m.

She switched legs and put her weight into the stretch until stiff muscles eased, and she was ready to run. She pounded down the sidewalk, heat reflecting up at her.

Four-foot-tall sandhill cranes strutted across the road. She usually enjoyed the birds' antics on her daily run through the campus. Not today. Today she needed to eliminate her frustration with the Army's response to last night's theft.

"Sit tight," they'd said. "Don't tell anyone about it, and we'll get someone in place to help as soon as possible."

Sit tight, my eye. Not when someone had stolen the software and one of her prototypes, putting six years of work in jeopardy.

Typical military response. Usually she was grateful to have such a prestigious job at thirty-one, and she loved working with this dedicated group of men and women. But today reminded her of the hassles of partnering with the military. The brass rarely told her what she needed to know until they believed she needed to know it. Aggravating to say the least.

Forget about it. Move on.

She tried to empty her mind. Reframe her thinking. Move into a better frame of mind to lead her team. She increased her pace beyond her normal routine and plunged into a secluded parking area with taller trees blocking the sun.

Good. The darkness matched her mood and her disappointment.

How many man-hours had she put into the helmet-mounted display and software to provide a fully immersive virtual training system? A system that simulated a variety of environments facing foot soldiers. Mountains, trees, deserts, jungles. Most everything they would face. All with the hope of saving lives with realistic training that was now endangered if the Army didn't act fast and recover the prototype.

Her project killed before it even had a chance to live.

Angry, she rounded a corner and pushed herself until she neared the end of the loop and her lungs screamed for oxygen. She would soon complete the loop and be back at the institute.

Then what? Her thoughts were still a jumbled mess. She couldn't face her staff this unsettled. They would ask questions, and she had to hide the theft for now.

She ran in place. Breathed deeply of the thick, steamy air. Stared over a small pond.

A hand came out of nowhere and clamped over her mouth. An arm snaked around her chest, pulling her back against a solid wall of muscle. Winded, she barely had the strength to breathe, let alone fight, but instincts kicked in. She jabbed an elbow to the man's gut.

No response. Nothing. He didn't even grunt.

She stomped on his foot and elbowed him again.

He tightened his grip, clamping her arm against her body and dragging her backward. She dug her heels in the thick St. Augustine grass trying to gain purchase and slow their progress.

No change.

Her heart thumped an irregular beat as panic skittered over her spine.

The man increased his speed, moving quickly down the slope toward the pond.

Alligators. No, no, no! Not this.

He drew her closer to the water. Step after step. The sour, organic smell alerted her to the pond's nearness. Movement on the pond. In the distance. The telltale bony armored plates of a gator's back so common in Florida. The creature glided through the water. Sending out ripples over the surface. His elongated head a forewarning of what was to come.

Oh, God, no! Please, no!

Fear twisted her stomach.

How could she have let this happen? Especially now?

She'd screwed up. Let her thoughts of the theft distract her. The colonel had warned her that the thief could be coming after her. The very reason she ran on campus with added security instead of at home this morning. But she'd relaxed. Trusted in security and failed to follow basic Self-defense 101. Prevention.

After her former boyfriend Travis had learned she jogged alone, he'd taught her skills to stay safe. To know the area. Know her exact location and listen for anyone approaching. Know her escape routes.

Travis. What would he tell her to do?

Her mind raced as her captor skirted around the pond. *Good.* Away from the gator now nearing shore. A moment of relief surged through her. He dragged her toward a parking lot. A van waiting.

This guy wasn't going to kill her. He was abducting her.

No. No. Act. Do something.

Panic claimed her mind, leaving nothing but fog.

Do something. Think, Claire, think!

Drop your weight, Travis had said. Bring the attacker down and elbow his head.

Do it. Now!

She fell forward and jutted both elbows upward. He budged but very little and jerked her upright then continued moving. She dug her heels into the grass. Tried to slow him down. No good. Her efforts didn't faze him.

He approached the deserted parking lot. The white cargo van. The side door open like a waiting prison cell.

No. Oh, no.

If he wrestled her into the van, she might never come out. But how did she stop him?

Travis had shared a last-ditch tactic with her. It would be painful and might knock her out, but she had nothing to lose.

Nothing!

She flopped as far forward as possible and with her remaining strength threw herself back, ramming her head into his face. Her skull connected with his jaw and her glasses flew from her face. Pain sliced through her head.

He grunted, but kept moving.

No.

She slammed him again. Saw stars. A black tinge colored the edges of her vision, already blurred without her glasses.

God, no. Please. Give me strength.

One more try. One more. She had to succeed. Her life depended on it.

She dipped forward and roared back. Her head connected hard. She stomped his foot and elbowed him at the same time. The perfect trifecta, making his arm slacken. With a burst of adrenaline, she spun free and bolted toward the road.

Without her glasses, the trees ahead swam before her

eyes, but she dug deep and raced on. She couldn't hear his footfalls behind her, but she sensed him chasing her. He was big with powerful, long legs and was likely gaining on her.

Look back. Check.

No. No. It will only slow you down.

Pain razored up her legs. Her lungs screamed for air. Her entire body begged to crumple onto the thickly matted grass. But she didn't. She kept going.

Down an incline. Up the other side. Along another pond. Her foot sank into slimy wet muck. She catapulted to the ground.

His hand clamped her ankle like a vise.

She screamed and kicked free. She grabbed the thick grass to gain her footing. She righted herself and kicked out with every ounce of energy, connecting with his shoulder and leaving him prone. She charged up the incline.

"Help," she screamed but stopped. Better to save her breath for running.

She picked up speed. Kicking it into the highest gear her fatigue allowed.

Closer and closer to the road. Closer to help. To the faint hint of traffic sounding in the distance.

You can make it. You can make it, her mind chanted with every step until she believed it.

She ran every day. She was fast. She could outrun this creep and flag down help before he caught her. She really could. She had to.

She was racing for her life.

2

_____

Travis turned the corner to the institute and spotted an ambulance and three police cars blocking the entrance flanked with tall palm trees. He couldn't see far enough ahead to figure out what was going on, but his gut said Claire was in trouble.

He offered a quick prayer on her behalf and pulled to the side of the road. Slapping on his beret, he got out and jogged down the street. The intense Orlando humidity and heat hit him in the face, making it hard to breathe. He'd once joined Claire in her daily run when he'd worked with her, but she was accustomed to this weather. He might live in North Carolina, but he still struggled with the intense humidity.

A burly male police officer manning a barricade near the entrance flipped up a beefy hand and pulled back his shoulders, straining the seams on his uniform. "No one goes in."

Travis swallowed his anxiety and forced out a smile. "Can't you make an exception? I'm late for an appointment."

"Like I said, man. No one goes in."

The urge to ignore his command and push on had Travis

taking a step, but he couldn't help Claire if he was arrested. "My CO will have my hide if I don't make my meeting. You know what happens when you fail to complete orders, right? Couldn't you ask whoever's in charge if I can slip through?"

The cop waffled for a moment then nodded. "Wait here."

After he moved out of view, Travis jumped the barricade. He rounded the ambulance with lights twisting into the bright sunshine and stuttered to a stop as he sought to make sense of what he was seeing.

Claire sat on the sidewalk, her head lowered. She was dressed in running gear, with most of her ponytail ripped free, leaving honey-blond strands jutting out like porcupine quills. Raw, ugly sores marred her knees, and she rubbed her hands over her arms as if trying to rid herself of something horrible. Perhaps she heard his approach, because she suddenly raised her head.

Emotions flashed around them as bright as a detonated charge in the black of a Saharan desert night while the nearby chaos faded into the background. Travis knew returning to the institute again would be hard. But this? Seeing Claire wounded and afraid ripped a hole in his gut. The vague sound of footsteps sounded behind him—the cop coming to haul him away—and somehow, he got his feet moving toward Claire again. He took off his beret and tucked it into his belt.

"Hello, Claire," he said, making sure to keep a level tone when a vise clamped down on his gut.

She squinted at him, her gaze sharpening. "Just when I thought the day couldn't get any more difficult, they send you."

Under normal circumstances, he knew she wouldn't say such a thing. She wasn't mean, far from it, but shock must be pulling her uncensored feelings to the surface.

And the words lacerated him, proving she could still inflict serious pain. The only woman in his thirty-three years on this earth who could do such damage.

"Do you want me to haul him away?" the cop asked.

Travis braced himself for Claire's affirmative response, but she shook her head.

"Suit yourself." The cop's footsteps receded, but Travis wasn't alone with Claire for long.

A woman dressed in khakis and a blue polo shirt came to stand behind Claire. Travis blocked out the twenty-something woman and squatted in front of Claire.

"She was attacked," the other woman said, obviously reading his questioning expression.

"Attacked? How? Where?" he asked, barely able to stop himself from sweeping the only woman he'd ever loved into his arms.

"On her run," the woman answered. "She got away and managed to crawl back here."

Claire gestured at the woman. "Meet my new assistant, Dr. Julie Dickson."

"And you are?" Julie's narrow-eyed gaze ran over Travis.

"This is Captain Travis Chapman." Claire might as well have tossed a bucket of ice water over his head for as cool and disapproving as her tone came out.

"Travis?" Julie's eyebrows rose. "He's the... Oh, no! Oh... This isn't good, is it?"

Claire flashed a calm smile at her assistant. "Would you mind going inside and telling the team I'm okay so they don't worry?"

"Sure." Julie bit her lip for a moment. "I mean if you're sure you want me to leave you alone with...him."

"Go. I'm fine." As Julie departed, Claire ran a finger up the bridge of her nose, likely trying to adjust glasses that had fallen off in the attack. The gesture was classic Claire when she was stressed or uneasy. Despite her claim that she was fine, she obviously needed comfort. Comfort she'd once sought from him. He scooted closer. Her eyes flared with attraction for a moment before she forced it away.

Interesting. She wasn't as immune to him as the day she'd claimed her job was her one true love.

Right. That day. The day she rejected his proposal. They'd devoted nearly every waking hour to CATS, but once his part of the work was done, he'd known he would return to base in North Carolina, and he didn't want to leave Claire behind. He was ready to make a real commitment, to build a future with her...but he should've seen the rejection coming. All that mattered to her was honoring her father. After his death in a military chopper crash, she wanted to make his dreams of a better training system for soldiers come true, and that meant her job came first.

Always.

She started picking at grass clinging to her socks, but she was such a mess it made little difference. "I assume you're here about the theft?"

"That and to serve as your protection detail. Guess I'm a bit late." Without thinking, he lifted his hand to move a stray strand of hair from her eyes, but she cringed.

Got it. Message received loud and clear. Nothing's changed between us, and keep my big mitts off.

"Your protection isn't necessary." She gestured at the surrounding commotion. "I'm sure with all the cops swarming around here my attacker won't be back."

"Sounds like you think this was a one-time thing and doesn't have anything to do with the theft."

She nodded but a flash of pain darkened her face, and she stopped moving.

Pain he would do anything within his power to take away. "Tell me what happened."

She took in a breath. Blew it out. Pulled in another. And out. "It was simple, really. I was running. A man came up from behind and tried to drag me to a van. I remembered your self-defense moves. Had to go all the way to the head butt, but I got away." She ended with a wry smile, easing the tense lines around her mouth for a moment.

"If your attacker was trying to abduct you, we need to assume that it was the thief after the information only you possess."

She looked him dead in the eye for the first time, her expression unreadable. "You think they've already figured out the prototype doesn't work, and they want to get the missing specs from me?"

He nodded. "And that's why I'll be with you twenty-four/seven until the thief is apprehended."

"No!" She shook her head hard, not even stopping when pain pinched her eyes tighter. "Not happening. So not happening."

He refused to let her words sting. He was here to do a job and that meant tuning out the personal and getting the job done. He would protect her no matter what she wanted.

Still, it would be easier if he gained her cooperation. "Making a snap decision isn't like you, Claire. Use that wonderful analytical brain God gave you. Set aside your emotions and weigh every aspect."

Her chestnut eyes met his and emotions raced through them so fast he couldn't tell what she was thinking.

"Okay, fine," she said, but crossed her arms. "You're right. Protection is probably a good idea, but the police can provide it."

Despite his frustration, he had to smile at her answer. He'd encouraged her to problem solve and she had. She just wouldn't accept the most logical solution.

"I can do a better job than the police." He didn't even try

to sound modest. "Besides, my CO has assigned me to your detail. You may be a civilian but you work for the Army. So, short of leaving your job, you have no choice in the matter."

"Not so fast. I'm sure your CO will entertain an alternative." She turned away and cupped her hands around her mouth. "Detective Purcell," she called out. "Can I have a word with you?"

A string bean of a man wearing a rumpled suit and holding a typical police-issue notepad headed their way.

Travis eyed her, searching for her motives, but failed. "I don't know what you're up to, Claire, but the theft is still on a need-to-know basis, and this guy or any other law enforcement officer doesn't need to know about it."

"Relax."

Right. How can I relax when the woman I once loved was mauled and barely escaped?

When her attacker was most likely to return?

When Purcell stood staring at Claire, she gestured at Travis. "My associate thinks this may not be a random attack and that I need protection."

"Not random, huh?" Purcell shifted to face Travis. "Care to share your reasoning?"

Travis would have to phrase his words to keep from giving away confidential information. "She works on a top-secret project worth millions, and someone might want to abduct her to gain access to it."

"Do you have any evidence suggesting a concrete connection?" Purcell asked.

"No, but my gut says she's still in danger."

"Can your department provide protection?" Claire asked, hope ringing through her tone.

Purcell frowned. "Without proof of an ongoing threat, we don't have the manpower for a detail."

Travis looked pointedly at Claire.

She held his gaze for a moment, her mouth set in a grim line. "Then welcome to Orlando, Travis," she said with unmistakable belligerence in her voice. "I'll accept your help, but that doesn't mean I like it."

∼

Travis wasted no time ushering Claire back into the building for safety. While she showered and changed clothes to bag them for the police, he found an empty conference room to call Colonel Vogler and bring him up to speed on the attack. "With an attempt to abduct Dr. Reed having already happened, I'd like to request additional support."

"Nothing else has changed, and I'm reluctant to provide anyone else. For every additional person read in on this theft, our chances of it getting out increases."

"Did the team spin up last night?"

"Affirmative."

Travis socked a fist into the wall, jerking back as pain radiated up his arm. He'd forgotten Florida buildings were constructed with cinderblock. Not something he should shove a fist into. "What if we hired a civilian team to enhance my efforts?"

"Like who?"

"I have a buddy. Former SEAL. Has a company comprised of former spec ops guys and law enforcement officers. They train law enforcement personnel and handle in-depth investigations."

Vogler didn't respond right away. "Sounds like more people than we want to bring in on this."

"We could start with the company owner Gage Blackwell. I know he still has top-level security clearance if you're worried about that. Then as the investigation plays out, we add team members as needed. Getting clearance from you, of course, for each one."

"I don't know."

"Jackson Lockhart works for Blackwell," Travis said, naming a former Green Beret who'd reported to Vogler for years. "He wouldn't work for just anyone, and that tells you the quality of their operation."

"It does indeed. Was sorry to lose Lockhart to that knee injury." Vogler let the silence linger.

Travis resisted saying anything more and overplaying his hand.

"Send me details on this Gage Blackwell and his company," Vogler finally said. "I'll review the info, check into his clearance, and get back to you." Vogler ended the call.

Travis wasted no time dropping into the nearest chair and searched his phone for Blackwell Tactical to gather intel for Vogler. He copied Gage's bio, touting his many years as a SEAL. What he didn't mention to Vogler was that Gage had to retire from his SEAL team after an arm injury. Turned out for the best as his daughter Mia suffered a traumatic brain injury when she was in a car accident with her mom. Gage's wife died, and Mia now needed special attention that Gage could provide when he was out of the service and stateside all the time.

Travis added the bios for the other Blackwell Tactical team members to show the diversity of skills on the team. A former FBI cybersecurity professional, Portland Police Bureau sniper, Army Ranger, recon Marine, and of course, former Green Beret. Then he added the types of training they provided. Shooting on the move, concealed carry, close-quarter combat, handling long guns, survival skills, and cybersecurity and crime.

Finally, he added company reviews and a link to the

Better Business Bureau, then emailed the report to Vogler and marked it urgent.

He was tempted to call Gage to check his availability, but there was no need. Once a spec ops guy always a spec ops guy, and that meant supporting your team members. Now and forever. Sure, Travis and Gage were in different branches of the military, but they'd worked joint ops, which was how they'd met. They both considered each other brothers and would come to the rescue if needed.

To Claire's rescue in this case.

As if thinking about her brought her closer, she strode down the hall with Julie, deep in conversation. That worry line between Claire's brows remained in place.

He didn't like seeing it. Not one bit.

He wanted to erase the line and put a smile on her face. The only way he could do that was to recover the virtual device and stop the person who attacked her. Travis could have a go at it alone, but he would work faster with Gage's help. Not only in the investigation, but in protecting Claire.

Ignoring what was best for him, he got out his phone and tapped Vogler's phone number.

"This better be important, Chapman," Vogler said.

Despite the warning, Travis continued. "I'm checking to see if you got my email."

"Reviewing it now," Vogler said.

"Impressive team, right?"

"Yes," Vogler said.

"And Gage's clearance? You confirmed that okay?" Travis was bordering on insubordination in questioning Vogler, but if that was what it took to protect Claire he would do it.

"He could be read-in."

"You approve, then?"

Vogler let out a long breath. "I swear dealing with you

spec ops guys is like herding a bunch of toddlers sometimes."

"So you've said in the past," Travis said. "And yet, you know we'll come through for you every time. And if we're asking for something, we truly believe we need it."

"Fine. We'll hire Blackwell Tactical to assist in protection and investigation, but for now, Gage Blackwell is the only one in the know."

"Got it."

"And Chapman, if word of this theft gets out, I'll hold you personally responsible."

Travis opened his mouth to point out that the information could come from Claire or even the thief, but Vogler ended the call before Travis could get out a word.

Fine. Travis would need to warn Claire again, but first a call to Gage.

He dialed his friend's number.

"G-man," Gage said, using the nickname short for Green Beret that Gage had given Travis many years ago. "Been a long time, bro. You still active duty?"

The last time Travis had seen or talked to Gage was when Gage had wanted a reference on Jackson Lockhart. "Yeah. Lockhart working out for you?"

"Better than I could've hoped."

"Told you he was a strong operator."

"You did," Gage said. "I know you didn't call just to catch up. What can I do you for?"

"I hoped you'd like to take a trip to see the big mouse." Travis laughed over his Disney reference and explained his need in Orlando, leaving out any mention of his personal connection to Claire. "And if that's not intriguing enough, I'll bet Dr. Reed would be glad to have you run some training sessions with her prototype."

"When do you need me there?"

"Yesterday."

"I'll have my chopper pilot take me to Portland and can catch a red eye out of there tonight if there're seats available."

"Seriously. You have your own helo?"

"I do," he answered, pride of his accomplishment behind his words.

"I need to get out there and see this operation of yours."

"Just don't go getting injured because you want to work for the super team." Gage laughed, but Travis could tell it was forced. All of Gage's team members had to leave their former jobs due to injuries and weren't employable in their chosen fields anymore. Gage's team provided them challenging work when they might not find anything close to their prior jobs, but they all still had lost their chosen professions.

"I'll check the flights out and text you my plans," Gage continued.

"Thanks, man."

"You'd do the same for me."

"I would."

"Later, man." Gage ended the call.

Feeling a bit more optimistic about his assignment, Travis strode down the hall to find Claire and share the good news. Hopefully she wouldn't see Gage as a substitute for Travis's protection but instead as an enhancement.

If she tried to use this as an excuse to stay away from him, he didn't know what he might say or do.

3

Claire wanted to keep her clothing for the Veritas staff to process for touch DNA tonight, but she couldn't tell the police about the theft and that meant she had to hand the bag to the detective.

"Don't expect instant results," he said from where they stood inside the institute's front door. "Our lab is notoriously backed up, and they'll have to wait their turn in the queue.

She nodded but hoped the Army could find a way to speed them along.

"I've got men out canvassing the area," Purcell said. "Maybe we'll get lucky and have a witness to the attack. Or at least someone who saw the guy in the van. Or got the van's plates. Or even security camera feed of the vehicle."

"Other than the DNA that would be your only lead, right?"

He nodded. "Unless you've thought of someone who might want to try to abduct you."

She shook her head and hated lying to this honest, hardworking man. She didn't actually have a name of someone who might want to abduct her, but she did have a motive.

He fished a business card from his pocket and it was as rumpled as his jacket. "Call me if you think of anything, and I'll keep you updated on our findings. In the event this was a random attack of a man wanting to abduct a woman, we'll increase our patrols in the area. Until then, keep your eyes and ears open."

She nodded, and he stepped out, swinging the bag holding her favorite running attire. She would have to break in a new pair of shoes on her next run, truly the least of her worries. Now she needed to deal with her staff and get them on board with a testing schedule for Travis.

She made her way down the hall to their large conference room where they and Travis waited. They were deep in discussion over the sequence they wanted to follow in the testing. She hated tricking her team this way. Making them think his sole purpose for visiting was the testing. She didn't want to use them this way. She would really put him through the testing as much as she could. Starting this afternoon. Then she would use the results of his tests to make the software and prototype even better. That way she wasn't misleading the team—at least not as much. Sure, they might be mad when they found out about the theft, but hopefully she could explain it well enough to not ruin any relationships she'd built over the years.

She glanced around the room at the team's excitement over having a top-rated special operator testing the prototype. Travis seemed equally as interested. Or at least he was fully engaged, and for the first time since they'd laid eyes on each other again, his dark gaze wasn't locked on her.

She closed her eyes, hoping when she opened them he would be gone. But he was there. Being charming. Handsome. Captivating. Everything she remembered him to be and more—and everything she couldn't have.

Which is why she'd been terribly rude to him outside

and why she needed to keep her distance until she could figure out how to spend time with him and not open her heart again. That meant ending this meeting and sending him to the testing room. While he ran through several CATS simulations, she would gain time to process his arrival, and as a bonus, she would cement his cover story with her staff.

She clapped her hands. "Okay, people, let's get to it. Be sure to make Captain Chapman feel at home."

He came to his feet, his body radiating power and demanding attention, but he immediately disarmed her staff with a smile, much the same way he'd once disarmed her.

"Please." He directed a pointed look at Claire. "Captain Chapman is a mouthful. Call me Travis."

An intern posed a question, and Claire adjusted her spare pair of glasses to watch Travis answer. He held his shoulders back, accenting his flawless posture and the perfect fit of his dress uniform. Even after hours of travel, making phone calls while she'd showered and changed, plus sitting through this staff meeting, the green and khaki fabrics were still crisp and neat with perfect seams.

His dark brown, nearly black, strands were long enough on top that once upon a time she hadn't been able to keep her fingers out of them, and he had a close-cut beard in a matching color. He was allowed to go against standard regulations and have facial hair and longer hair to blend in on covert missions. Not that it mattered here, but maybe he'd just arrived stateside or was on the way somewhere else when this theft interrupted the deployment. If so, he was probably even less happy with the arrangement than she was.

Julie approached him, and his smile widened, one corner crookedly tipping higher. Claire remembered a similar smile when they'd first met. A smile that had made her feel as if she was the only person in the room.

Enough. An hour with the guy and you're instantly where you were two years ago.

She'd worked too hard to get over him, and she needed to remember he wasn't here because she'd suddenly decided their relationship was a good idea. He was here to make sure the thief didn't obtain the missing information and to recover the prototype.

She crossed the room and ignored the questions in Julie's eyes. As Claire's former roommate, Julie knew about Travis, but Claire hadn't met Julie until after the breakup, and she'd never heard the full story.

Claire forced herself to turn her attention to Travis. "You'll want to change for testing. Assuming you brought your ACU."

"Roger that." He lifted his stuffed duffle bag where apparently he'd planned ahead for testing and packed his Army Combat Uniform. He would wear the combat uniform to simulate real-life combat action.

Claire turned to Julie. "Would you show Captain Chapman to the locker room and then set up the testing gear?"

That's it. All business. Stay polite yet firm and you'll be okay.

"Sure," Julie said pleasantly. "Follow me." She set off for the door, but Travis didn't budge.

Instead, he leaned close and looked at her through solemn black eyes. A look she knew was the closest he would ever come to acknowledging she'd somehow hurt him. "Call me Captain Chapman instead of Travis one more time and there will be consequences," he said in a no-nonsense tone.

"I thought it best to keep things formal between us."

He met her gaze and held it, the hurt already fading.

"Try all you want, sweetheart, but calling me captain won't make our history go away."

She opened her mouth to argue, but there was nothing she could say. Plus, her team would question why she formally addressed him after his request to be called Travis.

"Fine. Travis it is." She jerked her head at the door. "Julie's waiting for you."

His serious expression gave way to a smile. "I know the testing's a ruse, but I'm jonesing to see how our plans came to life."

She didn't bother denying his claim to the project. His feedback and ideas had helped make CATS a supreme training tool and despite the drama between them now, she was thankful for his input. "Then your assignment won't be such a burden for you."

An eyebrow went up. Oh, man. He appeared as fierce as the virtual enemies she'd created for CATS. "Might be a good idea to try to solicit alibis for last night from your team while I test CATS."

She arched an eyebrow. "You really do believe the theft is an inside job, don't you?"

"Yes, and I'll keep on believing it until we prove someone broke in here." He held her gaze. "You never did tell me exactly how you discovered the theft."

"When I arrived, I went to open the cubby where we store the device prototypes."

"Yeah, I remember. Each device has its own cubby. You lock them up every night and only open the one that's in use or if it needs to be worked on."

She nodded. "If I'm on-site, which is most of the time, I take care of it. I was here last night so I know it was in the locked cubby when I left for the day. "

"Who else has a key?" Travis asked.

"Our security manager, but he's at a conference in Texas

so he couldn't have opened the cubby. I suppose someone could've gotten ahold of our keys, but they have a do not copy inscription on them and no reputable locksmith would duplicate them."

"Plenty of dishonest locksmiths out there," Travis said. "So when did you discover the software was downloaded?"

"The devices are worthless without the software, so I immediately went to look at the main file. It uses encryption and obfuscation techniques to stop unauthorized parties from reading, modifying, or reverse-engineering the software. The change log showed that it had been downloaded last night around eleven fifteen. I quickly called our security company, and they told me the system was offline for an hour around that time."

"And that's when you got the higher-ups involved?"

"I did, but I really wanted to have our IT staff review the network activity to see if the software was cloned. I resisted the urge because I didn't want word to get around and freak out my team."

"And then the top brass told you to keep it quiet."

"Yeah, which is where you came in, and why we still haven't gotten a look at the network logs."

"That'll all be taken care of when the Veritas expert arrives."

"If he can prove it's someone on my team, I really don't want to know who it is." She shivered. "But I know I have to."

"Which is why you need to question anyone you think has any possibility of being our thief." He took a few steps toward the door and then looked over his shoulder. "You never pull any punches, Claire. So try to be subtle in your questioning."

She planted her hands on her hips. "I can do subtle."

"I've never seen it, but then we pretty much went straight

to kissing and there's nothing subtle about that." He chuckled and strode away.

Ugh! She planted her hands on her hips and fumed inside. Julie continued to study her with the intensity that made her good at her job, but Claire wished she would let it go right now. She forced herself to relax. Wouldn't do to raise any suspicions. Not even romantic ones.

Travis was right. She was usually a plain talker. She needed to develop better acting skills fast, not only for Julie but for Travis too. To keep him from discovering that even though she'd ended things with him—and continued to believe she'd made the right decision—he still had the ability to make her head spin.

She went to her office, all the while trying to figure out a way to deal with everything. Julie. Travis. The theft.

Work. Focus. That's the only solution. And one that always worked.

At her desk, she first entered the information needed in the software to make it work for Travis's test. She would love to be able to trust someone else with the data, but it had prevented the software from falling into the wrong hands. She'd just never thought anyone would actually try to steal the software, putting her life in danger.

She opened a list of staff on her computer. The Army contracted her team and worked out of their research facility, but the team was made up of mostly civilians. She ran her finger over the screen and mentally made a list of the people who might have a motive to steal the device.

First, they had to fit her attacker's build. Second, she figured she was looking for someone with money issues. Even if it were an espionage-related theft, it could've been done for money. She came up with six possible suspects. Two of the guys were out of the building that afternoon, and one was no longer an employee. She would start with the three guys she would most likely find at their desks.

She grabbed her empty mug to head for the coffee pot next to Paxton Lyle's desk, where she would start a casual conversation. She wasn't sure the graphic designer had money issues, but he was always asking for a raise.

She swiped her card to access the department and strode toward him. He kept his head down, staring intently at his computer. Not unusual. Most of their staff got caught up in their work and wouldn't know if a bomb went off next to them. She made a point of making noise when she poured the coffee and started down the aisle between desks again.

He lifted his head, not a hint of interest in her actions on his face.

She stopped by his desk. "How's your day going?"

"Fine." His expression lit with suspicion.

She forced a yawn and raised her mug. "Need an afternoon pick-me-up. I was out too late last night. You do anything fun?"

The redhead leaned back, and his chair groaned with his weight. "Depends on your definition of fun."

"What'd you do?"

"Played World of Warcraft with my brother."

She was vaguely familiar with the MMORPG—massively multiplayer online role-playing game, but wasn't into online gaming. However, if he played with his brother he had a solid alibi. That was if he was still playing at eleven p.m. when the security system had been tampered with.

"I've heard that's an addicting game and it's hard to stop."

"Tell me about it." He let out a squeaky breath. "We were at it until two."

"You don't look tired like I do."

"What can I say? I don't need much sleep." His phone rang. "Gotta take this call."

She nodded, thankful to end their awkward conversation that proved Travis's point. She wasn't a shoot-the-breeze kind of person. Hopefully, she would do better with the next suspect, Doug Quigley, who worked in software quality assurance, where the team's water cooler was located. Claire took her cup back to her office and grabbed her water bottle. She slid her card again and stepped into the department. She lifted her water bottle for anyone who might be looking at her and walked down the aisle.

Doug yawned.

Claire couldn't ask for a better opening. She stopped by his desk, which was cluttered with action figures from Star Trek. "Late night."

"My brother's bachelor party." He scratched his blond beard that matched his long hair. "I should probably have taken today off, but we have a target date tomorrow. I need this job and didn't want to miss it." He crossed his arms and stared at Claire.

As usual, he pointed out that he needed his job, not that he liked working at the institute. The reason for her questioning, but it sounded like he had a solid alibi too.

"We appreciate your dedication." Claire held up her bottle again and made her way to the cooler.

She noticed that Lieutenant Kent Norton's office lights were still out, making him unavailable for interviewing. He believed he should have her job as program director, but as much as he'd wanted it, he didn't have as well-rounded experience as she did managing people. As a software engineer, he was a tech geek through and through and often made others outside of the IT department that he managed mad with his direct approach.

She filled her water bottle and scoped out suspect three's

desk. She shouldn't even have put Hector on the list. He didn't deserve it. He supported his mother and two younger siblings. Such an honorable thing to do. But it also meant he was always in need of money and worked every minute of overtime she could offer. And his mom had recently broken her hip, was living in a rehab facility, giving him bills to pay that he likely couldn't afford.

She strolled over to him and guilt ate at her even before her question came out. "How's your mother doing, Hector?"

Tired eyes looked at her. "As good as she can be."

"Looks like you were up late with her."

"Honestly, no." He took off his computer glasses and scrubbed a hand over his jet-black hair. "I had to take a second job to help pay the bills. Been working nights at the twenty-four-hour McDonalds by my house. Don't get in until three."

"I'm so sorry, Hector," she said and had to resist the urge to pat his arm. "I know that has to be hard on you. If I could increase your pay, I would."

"I know and I would never want to leave this job for more money," he said, his sincere tone so believable she hated her mission even more. "But don't be surprised if I have to do it. The bills are mounting."

She'd lost IT staff to big tech in the past. The only real benefit that kept many of her workers with her was top-notch, low-cost insurance. Didn't do Hector any good. His mother couldn't be on his plan.

Her phone chimed a text from Julie. *Testing in final mode.*

"I have to go," she told Hector. "I'll take another look at the budget to see if I can find anything extra for you, but even if I do, it won't be a big increase."

"Still, I appreciate that you care." He gave her a wide smile, his gleaming white teeth bright in his tan face. "You always do."

She nodded and rushed away before she spilled her guts and told him she wasn't being totally honest with him. Sure, she did care about him and his family and often asked about their well-being, but today she was a spy all the way, and she hated every minute of it.

How did Travis do it all the time? True, he hadn't developed a relationship with the people he encountered, and they were bad people, but still, she couldn't do it. Not long-term for sure.

She stepped into the large testing room and hung by the door. Wearing a helmet and CATS virtual device, Travis was crouched in the stealth mode of a cat hunting prey. He'd dressed in his Army Combat Uniform as discussed. She was intimately familiar with ACU specs from creating the simulations. It consisted of eight-pocket camouflage pants and a matching five-pocket jacket that they called a blouse, along with brown battle boots. Travis had dressed this way because it simulated combat more realistically.

He eased left then right, his balance perfect, his movements sure. Claire knew exactly what he was seeing—he was at the spot in the simulation that placed him on a rocky outcropping designed to resemble the mountains of Afghanistan.

She could easily imagine him in a real battle, though not necessarily in Afghanistan. The third Special Forces group concentrated on covert operations in sub-Saharan Africa. His alpha team was dropped into unfriendly countries and left to infiltrate groups and gather intelligence. They frequently lived as locals and operated without military support. That meant no uniforms, leaving them outside the jurisdiction of the Geneva Convention. The enemy could torture or kill them on sight.

A violent shudder raced through her. This was the very reason she'd broken off with him.

Keep that in mind when he turns those heart-stopping eyes on you.

He suddenly stood and lowered his rifle, indicating the segment had come to an end. He removed the helmet and put it on a rack. When he caught sight of her, a boyish grin spread across his face.

Her mouth threatened to reciprocate before she clamped down on her lips.

He jogged across the room, boots thumping on the tile floor. He grabbed her in a hug and swung her in circles.

She felt weightless. Spinning. The room moving. She caught her breath and enjoyed the ride.

After a few rotations, he put her down. He kept her loosely enclosed in his arms. "You did it, Claire. Really did it. Everything we talked about came to life before my eyes." His breath was warm on her neck before he leaned back, still grinning from ear to ear.

"What a rush!" His body fairly vibrated from adrenaline.

She let herself be caught up in his smile. To feel the strength of his arms around her again. To catch a whiff of the same minty soap he used. To feel protected and cherished. To feel everything she claimed she no longer wanted in her life.

He tweaked her nose as he'd often done when they were dating. "I'm so proud of you, honey."

She basked in his praise. Standing there. Not moving.

A noise sounded from the observation booth. Julie.

What was Claire doing?

She snapped to her senses and stepped free. "I'm glad you liked it."

"Liked it? I loved it! This will revolutionize training. We can give hands-on skills to young recruits on every base and save lives."

Right. Saving lives. That's why she'd embarked on this

research in the first place. Her career military father had often lamented losing green recruits and wished for better training. She hadn't been able to do anything to save him from a chopper crash, but she could fulfill his wish.

She took another step back for good measure, earning a raised eyebrow. Too bad. She had to stick to her convictions and finish the job. Not fall for a handsome soldier who looked mighty fine in his uniform.

"I need to review the testing results with my staff before they head home," she said, making sure her tone was all business. "They'll have questions for you, and it would do them good to see your enthusiasm for the project. Do you want to get changed first or come to the observation deck with me now?"

He leaned closer. "I'll change now. If everyone is going home soon, I can't leave you alone up there while I'm in the locker room."

She lowered her voice in case the recording was still on. "You can't honestly think someone will attempt to abduct me right here."

"It's not likely, but I'm not taking any chances."

Julie stuck her head out of the observation room. "You two joining us for the debrief?"

"I'll be right there," Claire called out.

She took a fortifying breath and then met Travis's gaze. "Get changed and meet us inside."

He saluted her and spun to leave.

She let out a long breath and slipped into the observation room.

Julie looked up from a computer monitor, the glow reflecting on her excited expression. "Check out these stats."

Claire reviewed Travis's simulation data and resisted beaming with pride. "He's good, isn't he?"

"Good? He's amazing. He made it all the way through

the simulation without taking any kill shots. No one else has even come close to that."

Kill shots. In real life, Travis came under fire all the time. The longer he served as a Green Beret, the greater likelihood he would be shot. Maybe fatally. The same way his teammate Jeter had been killed. Thankfully, Travis had been by her side working on the simulator instead of on that mission with Jeter—or Travis could've died too.

That's why she'd had to end things with him. She couldn't have another military officer come to her door with terrible news. Awful news. She couldn't survive another loss like that. No way. Impossible. Which meant she couldn't be with Travis.

No matter how much she loved him.

Not that she told him that. He might do something foolish like leave the Berets to be with her, and she knew he would grow to resent that decision. Or maybe he would try to dispel her fear and draw out the inevitable end to their relationship.

That couldn't happen. Not at all. Better to cut things off right then. So she'd looked for a reason he couldn't dispute. Her job was the answer. She really couldn't afford the distraction of a long-term relationship at that stage of the project, and she'd shared her need to focus on saving lives. She'd hurt him, but as a soldier, he couldn't dispute the necessity of her work. And she was still convinced she'd done the right thing.

And if you know what's good for you, you'll keep on letting him think the same thing.

"Why aren't you impressed?" Julie demanded.

I am, but I don't want to be. "Maybe we need to make the training scenarios more difficult."

"Hah!" Julie said. "One guy out of hundreds who've tested CATS succeeding at this level does not mean we need to make it more difficult. We simply need to appreciate Travis's incredible abilities. No wonder they sent him for the final test."

Claire didn't know how to respond without lying, so she clamped her mouth closed.

Julie's gaze zeroed in on her. "Looks like you're having a hard time with him being here."

"A bit," Claire said, as she didn't know if it was appropriate to talk about Travis with Julie when Claire was her supervisor.

A fine line they'd walked for some time now.

Claire had met Julie at a conference right after her break-up with Travis, and after common interests forged a friendship between them, they'd become roommates. Then Julie took a job at the institute, and Claire eventually became Julie's supervisor. Claire withdrew a bit from the relationship and tried to keep the most personal details of her life private. Luckily, it didn't affect Julie at all. She was such an easygoing person that she readily accepted the change in roles, but decided to get a place of her own when she started making more money.

Still, Claire often had to remind herself to hold back. Like now when Julie seemed genuinely interested and wanted to help.

Business, Claire. This is business.

Julie shifted in her chair. "I hope you didn't let that get to you and you sent Travis home for the day. We all want to and need to question him about the simulation."

"I'd never let my personal concerns get in the way of CATS." Claire hoped she sounded more convincing than she felt. "He'll join us after he changes."

"Ooh, back in his dress uniform, huh? That'll be no hardship for us."

"Julie! Eric wouldn't be too happy to hear you say that."

Julie wiggled her fingers. "He hasn't put a ring on it yet, so there's no harm in looking."

If only Claire could say the same thing, but she was certain looking would get her in all kinds of trouble that even with her best effort would be nearly impossible to avoid. Plus, she couldn't afford to be distracted now. It would take all of her focus to find the prototype. To keep it out of the hands of unscrupulous soldiers who, with the proper training, would pose a serious threat to U.S. armed forces.

And soldiers could die.

4

———————

Travis waited with a very quiet Claire in the conference room as the remaining staff packed to leave for the night. Veritas was due on site in an hour, and it would be his and Claire's job to make sure no one entered the facility and saw them processing forensics. To that end, once her team was gone, Claire would disable all key card access for the doors until after Veritas departed.

He hadn't had a chance to tell her about Gage who'd texted while Travis was changing to say he would arrive tonight at two a.m. Now was the perfect time to tell her.

He swiveled his chair to face her. "I have a buddy coming tonight to help with our investigation and your protection detail."

She cocked an eyebrow. "One of your teammates?"

"No." He explained.

"Will you pick him up at the airport?" she asked, her fingers taking a death grip on the edge of the table.

So she *was* afraid but had been putting on a brave front. Just like her to do so. To keep him at arm's length? Or maybe a defense mechanism. Either way, he didn't like seeing it.

Travis gave her a reassuring smile. "He'll need a vehicle to participate in your protection detail and rented an SUV."

She arched a brow. "Tell me the truth. Is this because you don't want to be in the same room as me?"

"What? No." He shook his head for emphasis. "It's because I honestly think I need help."

"Then why not someone from your team?"

"They spun up last night on an op I was supposed to be on."

"Then another team?"

"I didn't ask. Don't know the other guys real well, but I've worked with Gage in the past. We know each other's rhythms. Something that could mean the difference between life and death."

"You mean my life? My death?" Her voice squeaked.

"I think this prototype is highly valuable but only if the thief has you or your information. Which means it's a given that whoever took it will be coming after you. And after you give them the information they want, you have no value to them anymore."

Grim reality settled in her expression.

He leaned closer to her. "Sorry. I hate to be so blunt, but it's the truth. You need to recognize that so you do as we ask when we ask. No questions. Just compliance."

"I will. I promise." She clutched her hands together, her gaze flitting around the room.

He'd terrified her. Had to be done. She had to see the danger, but now that she did, he would lighten the mood. "Gage can pose as someone here to test the prototype too. Then we'll finally see that I'm a more superior operator than he is." He laughed.

She smiled—but it was forced.

"So is there anything unusual in your schedule for the next few days that I need to know about?"

"Not that I can think of." She tapped her chin. "Oh, wait. Saturday night we have a work party. It's the sixth anniversary of starting this project, and I planned a celebration to honor the staff."

Something every insider would know about. "Where is this event happening?"

"Local hotel."

"If this isn't resolved, I don't know if you'll be able to attend."

"Attending is not optional. I *will* be there."

"Then let's hope we have this guy in custody by then."

She nodded. "I have an appointment on Friday to finalize the facility set up. I can't miss that either."

Not a good idea. Not at all. "Can't you send Julie?"

"She's already going, along with her boyfriend Eric, who is doing the music for the party, but I need to be there too."

He would most likely forbid it, but he didn't need to do it tonight. "We can wait to decide on Friday if this isn't resolved by then."

"You really think you can solve it before that?"

"I sure hope so."

"I get it. Coming back here is the last thing you wanted to do and want to get back to your real life." She wrapped her arms around her body.

He couldn't argue with her, but he wouldn't admit it. His stomach rumbled, giving him the perfect change in subject. "I haven't had a decent Cuban sandwich since I was here last. Our favorite place still deliver?"

She nodded. "I can order it. I'm guessing you want your usual classic Cuban with a side of rice and beans and Jupina to drink."

He loved that she remembered how much he liked the sweet pineapple soda and sandwich Cuban immigrants brought to Florida. They'd often shared that particular meal

42

and longing surged through him for the easy relationship they'd once had. The relationship he couldn't manage to keep his mind off of.

How could a woman who stood five-five on tiptoes wreak such havoc in his life?

"Sounds perfect," he said, but had to get away to compose himself. He tossed his credit card on the table. "While you order, I'll go check to see if everyone is gone. Use my card to pay, okay?"

"Okay," she said, seeming distracted.

Despite the desire to know what she was thinking, he shed his jacket and hung it on the back of a chair. He rolled up the sleeves of his khaki dress shirt and then went into the hallway. Jerking his tie loose, he inhaled deeply and blew out his tension before making a circle of the building, checking every office, conference room, and restroom. Empty.

He went back to join Claire, who was staring into the distance and didn't seem to notice him enter the room.

"All clear," he said, not pleased that she wasn't being vigilant. Or maybe she was just ignoring him. "I'll text my Veritas contact that they're clear to process the property. Maybe they can start early."

"I'll disable logins." She silently moved to the computer.

He located Sierra Byrd's phone number, the trace evidence expert, and told her the place was ready for them.

Finishing dinner. Will be there in 30, came her reply.

The landline rang. Adrenaline surged through his veins, and his hand automatically shot to his holstered weapon.

Claire grabbed the phone and listened. "Let him through."

Ah, right. Had to be the guards asking about the delivery person bringing their dinner.

"Dinner?" he asked.

She nodded.

"I'll get it." He motioned for Claire to stay put and headed for the door.

When they were seated at the table, food in front of them, he bit into the sandwich of slow-roasted pork, ham, Swiss cheese, then pickles, pressed on a grill. He groaned at the tangy sauces.As he swallowed, he searched for a safe topic. "Did you have any luck discovering alibis while I was having fun with CATS?"

She set down her sandwich and wiped her mouth, taking her time as if she didn't want to talk about the theft. "Not a lot. Since my attacker obviously wasn't a woman, I started with the guys on the team."

"You can't rule the women out. They could've hired a guy or teamed up with someone they know." He took a huge bite of his sandwich and savored the tangy flavor.

She frowned. "I hadn't thought of that. I'll review the list again tomorrow and talk to any women I come up with."

"What did the guys tell you?"

"Not much." She grabbed her drink but held it away from her mouth. "You, of all people, know how men can be about engaging in small talk."

"What, me?" He jabbed his thumb into his chest. "I can be social."

She rolled her eyes and took a long swig of her drink. "Only when forced."

"Okay, granted, I'm not big on small talk, but I speak when it's important."

"That you do." She stared over his shoulder, maybe lost in their past.

He knew better than to pursue that and quickly moved on. "So, no luck at all then?"

"I talked to three guys and ruled them all out." She lifted her sandwich.

"And your team's what...thirty people, give or take? It would take too long to talk to them all, so we should prioritize a list of people with motives. It's most likely about money but could be about revenge too. Either revenge on you or the Army."

"I figured the same thing and made a short list of guys to talk to first. I have six suspects. Only three were in the building today, and those are the guys I talked with."

"Good. Then let's expand your list to include any other motive you can think of. They would also need the ability to disable the security system and cameras, or alter the footage, and download the software."

"Doug and Hector fit that criteria, but they gave me solid alibis. They'll need to be checked out though. As will Paxton's alibi, though he's a graphic designer, and I don't know if he could disable the security system."

"Then they stay on the list until we confirm the alibis. Anyone else who you think has money issues that you didn't talk to?"

She grabbed a pen and legal pad and started writing names and alibis. He finished off his sandwich in a large bite and waited for her to finish.

"I don't like adding this next one." Her hand hovered over the yellow pad as she fidgeted with the pen, twisting it in and out of slender fingers. "Alan Babbit. His wife is undergoing experimental cancer treatments not covered by insurance, which means he's short on cash. He's a civilian hire. Hardware specialist and department manager. He'd be able to modify security. Plus, he fits my attacker's physical build, and he wasn't in the office at the time of my attack."

"Good." Travis tapped the notepad. "Put him on the list."

"I don't like questioning a guy who's going through so much, but I agree he has to be on the list." She jotted his name down and clicked the pen several times before adding

Kent Norton to the page. "Kent's a lieutenant who was passed over for my job. He's on the team, but he still complains about having a civilian in charge. He was also out of the office this afternoon, and he's the right size."

"So revenge might fit him. Does he have any money issues?"

She shrugged. "He came into an inheritance not long ago and used it to purchase a condo by Lake Eola."

"Whoa. He must've gotten a huge chunk of money," Travis said as he recalled the expensive historic housing near Orlando's famous Lake Eola fountain. "We'll stick with revenge, then. He might want to get back at you and the Army."

"Maybe me, but I don't know about the Army. He seems like he lives for his career, but you never know, right?"

"Right." Travis slurped the last of his drink. "Anyone else come to mind?"

Claire lifted her face to the ceiling. He should look away, but he couldn't take his eyes off the sleek lines of her throat. He knew firsthand how soft her skin felt. He shoved his hands into his pockets. He didn't care if keeping his hands in his pockets violated the uniform policy. The rule was so ingrained that it felt wrong and the discomfort distracted him from Claire.

She lowered her head, eyes awash with apprehension.

"Did you come up with someone else?" he asked, her concern making him dread the answer.

"Maybe...I don't know." She paused and bit her lip. "There's this guy. He's not on the team anymore, and his security access has been revoked. He probably couldn't pull off the theft."

"Would he have knowledge of the security system and the technical skills to alter it?"

"Yes. He's a software engineer."

"Maybe he could bypass it, then. Tell me about him."

"His name's Mike Robb. He's retired Army. Delta Force. He worked for us as a civilian. He kind of had a thing for me. It got to be a problem, and I had to fire him."

Travis's intuition sat up and took notice. A spec ops guy with stalker intent lifted his concern to a new level, but he played it down.

"A thing?" he asked casually to hide his unease.

"Okay, maybe it was more than a thing." She clenched her hands and took a deep breath. "His interest crossed the line and became an obsession. When his performance suffered at work, I had to let him go. That was about three weeks ago."

Travis's gut started churning, the sandwich he'd just enjoyed sat like lead in his stomach. "Have you seen him since then?"

"Sort of. I mean, he's called me and shown up here a few times since I let him go. Plus, I often run into him when I'm out. I suppose he could be following me."

"And you're just mentioning him now?" Travis's words shot out like an accusation before his chest constricted.

She eyed him for several moments, her cool expression in direct opposition to his turmoil. "After I was attacked this morning, I considered telling the cops about him. But then you were so certain the attack was related to the theft. Mike is off the team, and I thought it wasn't important to the investigation."

Travis sat forward and resisted the urge to shoot to his feet and pace away his anxiety. "I don't care if he's involved in the theft or not. He's bothering you, and I intend to have a word with him."

"Why?"

"He's stalking you, for crying out loud. That's not okay." He jerked his hands free and slammed a fist on the table.

Claire jumped, and he regretted the loss of control, but he doubted any man who'd once loved a woman could hear about a man potentially stalking her without exploding.

Breathing deeply, she stared at him while endless seconds passed. He wanted to beg her to speak, but he waited and cringed inside over her upcoming answer.

"Let's be clear about one thing, Travis," she finally said, dead calm in her tone. "Your assignment doesn't involve my personal life. Any problems I'm dealing with that aren't connected to the theft are none of your business."

"Fine. Leave the fact that he's obsessed with you out of this." Travis grabbed the pen and wrote down Mike Robb's name in big, bold letters, then circled it with a thick slash of the pen. "He's got a personal vendetta against you for firing him. In my mind that makes him our primary suspect, and I intend to have a conversation with him ASAP."

"Okay," she said, still calm and detached.

Unbelievable. How could she be so relaxed? More important, how could she keep this from him all afternoon? This guy was the perfect suspect. Or maybe Travis wanted Robb to be guilty because he was interested in Claire.

Interested, my foot. He's a stalker. Plain and simple.

Travis gave in to the need and got up to pace. He would spend the night researching Robb. Maybe ask Gage to have his cyber person do the same thing. But one thing he would do for sure. After dropping Claire off here tomorrow, he would go talk to the guy.

All right, maybe he'd do more than talk, even if Robb wasn't the thief. Travis didn't care what Claire said. He'd let the jerk have it for bothering her.

And if Robb turned out to be the thief after all? Then he was an imminent threat to the woman Travis would do just about anything to protect, and he would stop at nothing to keep her safe.

5

Claire instantly liked Sierra Byrd, but Travis seemed wary of the entire team. The Veritas partner and trace evidence expert had dishwater blond hair below her shoulders and thick bangs, and she was several inches taller than Claire's five-five. She wore a blue polo shirt with Veritas Center engraved on the chest and khaki cargo pants, as did the other partner who'd arrived with her. Nick Thorn, their computer and cybercrime expert, stood over six feet tall, was built, and had brownish hair with a matching close-cut beard. He was more detached than Sierra.

"If you'll show us to the computer where you think the software was downloaded, we'll get to work," he said, all business.

Claire blinked at him. "I have no idea where it was downloaded."

"Okay, so no preliminary investigating done then."

"I was instructed by Army brass to hold off to keep from letting word get out about the missing device." She crossed her arms, feeling the need to go on the defense with this guy.

Nick tilted his head. "How did you learn the device was

stolen and not just misplaced?"

She explained how they locked up the equipment at the end of every day.

He gave a sharp nod. "What did you do after you discovered it was missing?"

She shared how she checked the software and called the alarm provider. "They did say there wasn't an employee code assigned to the time it was disabled."

"So they didn't use a key card for access, but they must've actually interfaced with the system itself." Nick tapped his index finger on the table.

"Yeah," she said. "Which could also mean they disabled the locks on all of the doors as well as security cameras, and we won't have a log for their entry into any of the departments or video. I was hoping we would see a card swipe for the equipment room but it doesn't seem likely."

"I'll check the logs, but don't hold your breath."

She nodded when she really wanted to scream in frustration. "I also took a quick look at the doors and locks. I didn't see any physical damage from someone prying them open."

"Doesn't mean there isn't any," Sierra said. "We'll process the doors for prints, and I'll give the locks a more thorough examination to see if they've been picked."

"You can actually see that?" Claire asked.

Sierra nodded. "Using a pick tool on a lock is invasive. The pick tool is made of a stronger material than the softer brass or nickel-silver of lock components and will most always leave picking marks. The deeper or more pronounced the marks, the less skilled the picker. Of course, we can't tell if it happened now or at an earlier date, but we can most likely confirm the picking."

"Could the thief simply have stayed in the building after closing?" Nick asked.

Claire shook her head. "We have motion sensors, so I don't see how."

"Either way, our suspect needs skills to disable the system. Could be someone in your IT group." Nick scowled.

Travis took a step closer. "The look on your face says IT guys are worse than others."

"The average Joe could have enough knowledge to make changes, but not cover their tracks. IT professionals would know to hide their changes by modifying the logs." He smirked. "The good news is they almost always forget to change every area, and I catch them that way."

"You sound confident." *Cocky actually.*

"I have a pretty good success rate, so yeah, I guess I am." Nick laughed. "First it would be good to figure out which terminal they used to download the information. If I wanted to steal software and worked here, I sure wouldn't do it on my own computer. I'd use someone else's if I wanted to try to set them up or a computer that everyone has access to. Do you have such an animal?"

"Yes," Claire said. "In the conference room."

"Then we'll start there. I'll get an image running of that hard drive while Sierra begins processing the area."

Sierra gave an agreeable nod. "I'll also need to get my assistant and other techs working the area where you stored the prototype."

"Let me get the image going first." Nick shifted a large backpack on his shoulders. "It could take several hours to complete."

Sierra smiled at him. "Of course."

Claire appreciated how they worked together and didn't seem to let egos get in the way. She led them to the conference room, and Travis followed.

Nick stopped at the doorway. "Your rooms aren't secured?"

"Not our conference rooms but each department is secured with key card access only."

"I would recommend you rethink that," he said. "Any area where you have a computer should be secured."

Claire tried not to bristle at his insinuation that they hadn't done their job to protect their assets, but she took a step back. "Other than the computer, there's nothing to steal in here."

"On the contrary." He set down his backpack and took latex gloves from an outside pocket. "If the computer has access to your network server then there's valuable data and files to be stolen."

"But only employees can get in the conference room unescorted, and they could also steal it by using their own computer."

"Sure thing, but logging onto their device and onto any files on the server would create a record that would tie back to them." He put on the gloves, snapping them loudly in place. "If you had the door secured, they would have to sweep their security key cards to get into the room, thus creating another record."

"Unless they disabled the entire system like we think happened here," Travis pointed out.

Nick narrowed his eyes. "Still, they most likely found another way to log in or stole a co-worker's login to use in here. If not, we could solve this thing tonight."

"I'll see about making the change," she said. "But the prototype room has a key card, so if the whole system wasn't disabled, maybe we really can end this now by checking that log."

"I'll get this image going first." He shifted to look at his backpack, his brown eyes alive with the thrill of a hunt. "And I'll need an administrator's login to your network. Can you provide that or do I need to get it from someone else?"

She managed passwords for staff and issued them too. "I can provide it."

"Then go ahead and show Sierra and her staff to the room. I'll find you when I need you." He sat behind the computer and flicked his fingers in the air, clearly dismissing them.

She stepped into the hallway, Nick still on her mind. She didn't like to stereotype people, but he had an abrupt personality. Something she'd come to associate over the years with fellow IT staff. They didn't mean to be rude or abrupt. They were just more at home with computers than people. And isn't that what she wanted right now? A person who spoke computer languages and could find their thief, not some charming guy?

Sierra joined Claire. "Ignore Nick's behavior. He can forget his manners when he has a crime to solve."

"I only hope he can find something to help."

"He will," she said, her openness just the opposite of Nick. "He might be full of himself at times, but he has a reason to be. He's the best at what he does."

"Then let's hope he finds something to help us resolve this theft," Claire said as she led the way to the storage room at the far end of the building.

She swiped her card over the reader, and the door popped open. She held it for Serra and Travis. The overhead light sensor caught their entry and flooded the room with crisp blueish lighting.

"The prototype devices are stored in the large cabinet across the room," Claire said. "Each cubby is numbered to coordinate with the model."

Travis marched over there and studied the doors.

"Don't touch anything," Sierra warned.

Travis held up his hands. "Didn't plan on it."

"You'll need keys." Claire fished them from her pocket

and gave them to Sierra. "Second cubby on the left is the empty one."

"Separate key for every lock?" Sierra asked.

Claire nodded, wishing Nick were here to see their added security. "We wanted to make it harder to get at all the devices at one time."

"How many prototypes are there?" Sierra unlocked the main door to the cabinet and then the empty cubby inside of it.

"Two with our current specs." She pointed at the other door holding their current model. "The rest of the cubbies hold older versions."

Sierra cocked her head. "Wonder why they didn't take both of them."

Claire hadn't thought of that. "Good question."

"They took number two," Travis said. "Perhaps they thought you wouldn't notice the second one missing for a few days."

Sierra bent closer to the cabinet. "Surfaces are smooth and flat. Should enable us to lift clear prints."

Nick rushed into the room, his gaze searching until he fixed it on Claire. "Why didn't you tell me you used dummy terminals?"

"I didn't know it was a dummy," she said, not liking his tone.

"What's a dummy?" Travis asked.

"The monitor connects directly to the network, which acts as an input/output device for the terminal. So every action is handled by the server and not a hard drive on a PC. No hard drive means nothing for me to copy. I need immediate access to the network."

"This is good news for me." Sierra gave Nick a pointed smile. "I can get my guys on processing that room now."

"Yep," Nick said, his attention still on Claire. "Can you

issue that password now?"

She looked at Sierra. "Do you need anything else from me?"

"We're good to get started." She smiled. "I'll find you if I need anything else."

Claire nodded and then spun to leave for her office. Multiple sets of footfalls trailed behind her, and she assumed Nick and Travis followed. She sat behind her desk while the men stood over her on the other side. Nervous under Nick's scrutiny, she located the correct program to create a login and password for him. She jotted the information on a sticky note.

"Looks like you don't have two-factor authentication for that program." His deep tone declared what he thought of that.

He was talking about when a person attempted to log into a program and the software provided an authentication code to confirm the identity of the person logging in.

"We don't," she admitted.

"You really need to add it. Someone could have stolen your login details to create a new network login. Odds would be much lower if they had to confirm access on a phone or computer." He eyed her.

"Budget constraints," she said. This theft would hopefully force the Army to cough up more money for them to upgrade their systems. She would have a serious talk with their security manager about it. "If that happened, you should be able to see the login used to create these new credentials."

He nodded. "And then we can compare it to the legit logins to see if we can track the thief that way."

"At least that's good news," she said, hoping to eliminate the scowl on his face.

But he continued to watch her, his mouth turned down.

"Tell me at least none of you can access your computers without a password."

"We can't," she said, still feeling inept even with her degree in IT. "Once you finish, would you mind giving me a list of security improvements we should make? I can review it with my manager and fight for the funds to increase the level."

"Be glad to." His expression softened. "I know I'm coming on strong. Sorry about that. Security and prevention is my passion, and I don't pull any punches. I can't say if you implemented these security features that the theft would've happened or not. Depends on your thief's skills. But I like your attitude about wanting to improve."

She appreciated the backhanded compliment. "I don't ever want this to happen again."

"I get that for sure." He actually smiled. "Now if you'll show me to your server room, I'll get started on rooting out this thief."

She handed him the sticky note.

He studied it and gave a nod of approval. "At least you're using very strong passwords. Letters. Numbers. Caps. Symbols. All random and long. Would be hard to crack them." His eyebrow went up, and his approval morphed into pursed lips. "Which likely means the thief had your information."

"Impossible." She crossed her arms. "I take great care in not sharing my passwords with anyone. Not even my assistant."

He arched an eyebrow. "Ever log into your computer when one of your staff members is in the room with you?"

"Well, yeah, but—"

"Do you attempt to hide your keystrokes?"

"Not really."

"So it's possible someone saw the keys you pressed."

"I suppose, but—"

"But you can't imagine anyone who works with you doing that?" He leaned forward and tapped his finger on her desk. "Corporate espionage is rampant in our country, Dr. Reed. Particularly when it comes to stealing trade secrets. Just because you're a small company and know all the people who work for you doesn't make you immune to that —as is likely evidenced by the theft."

"You're right. I need to stop trusting so easily. To put your additional security measures into place and be sure I hide my login when I sign into my computer." Her face flaming from the embarrassment of her failure, she stood. "But right now we need to focus on finding this thief, not chastising me."

"Sorry," he said, making solid eye contact. "Don't be embarrassed. I find more lax security than you have in many places I investigate."

"That's something, I guess," she said, but didn't really believe it.

Expecting another scolding for something they'd done wrong, she led the way to the small server room at the back of the office space. She didn't come here often, leaving the hardware to her manager, and didn't know the details of how everything was connected, but she could figure it out as she assumed Nick would do.

She swiped her card and held the door for him. Air in the room kept chilly for the equipment rushed out and cooled her flushed face.

"Nice setup." Nick brushed past her to head straight for a computer terminal and plopped onto the chair.

Travis stopped next to her. "Stop blaming yourself. You didn't install the security."

"But I should've asked for more details. Not trusted as much."

He brushed his hand against hers. "You can't know every detail, and now that you have recommendations, I know you'll make sure they're implemented."

"I will." Budget was tight. Really tight, and without additional funding, upgrading would be a challenge, but she would find a way to do it. Unfortunately, that could mean Hector would be out of luck on his raise.

Help me to do both. Hector deserves more money, and we have to make the security changes. But then You know that.

She hoped God heard her. But did He? She wasn't sure. Not with the challenges she'd faced on the job to bring this software and hardware to production. But why would God not want the American military to be well-trained and reduce loss of life? No reason she could think of, but then she wasn't all-knowing like He was.

"I'm in," Nick said, his fingers flying over the keyboard.

She should be as excited as he sounded, but she dreaded the news he would bring to her. Would he tell her someone she counted on, trusted, and saw every day was a traitor?

"You can go now," he said, not looking up. "I'll let you know if I need anything else."

As much as she wanted to learn the thief's identity, she was glad to go. "This door will lock when it closes. If you leave you won't be able to get back in."

"Then be sure you pay attention to your phone in case I need you," he said without losing a beat.

Travis opened the door for her.

In the hallway next to him, she stepped back to wait for the door to latch.

"Intense and focused guy," Travis said. "I wouldn't take anything he says personally."

"Hard not to, but he seems like he knows what he's doing," she said, trying to focus on the positive. "Let's check in with Sierra again to see if she needs anything."

They found her still in the conference room at the computer terminal. She was lifting a wide strip of tape from the keyboard. She pressed it onto a card, grabbed a pen and began writing on the back of it.

She looked up. "Hey. I'm finding a lot of prints, but that's not surprising on a computer used by all of your staff."

Travis frowned. "Likely one of the reasons our thief decided to use it."

Sierra nodded. "I realize this operation is on a need-to-know basis, but if you want me to match names to the ones I lifted, we'll need to get prints from your staff."

Finally, something Claire could help with. "To work here, you have to be fingerprinted to pass a background check, and we have them on file for each employee."

"Oh, good. Get me a copy of all of them." Sierra filed the card in a small box. "We'll have to manually compare the prints we lift to them, and that will take longer than our usual searches of criminal databases. But since your employees won't have records searching those databases won't likely help. We'll do it anyway. Never know, we might discover we're looking at an outside suspect."

"What about my prints?" Travis asked. "I haven't touched the computer, but I have touched equipment in the building."

"Your prints are in Army databases, but we can't always access military records on a timely basis. It would be easier if you let me print you right now."

"Of course."

She reached into the field kit she'd carried into the room and took out a small zipped case. She drew out a device a bit larger than a cell phone but much thicker. She tapped the screen a few times and then turned it around to face Travis. "We'll do a full set, so press all four fingers of your right hand on the screen."

Travis complied, and the screen came alive to record them.

"Now your other four fingers," Sierra said.

Travis switched.

"Finally your thumbs."

He pressed his thumbs on the reader.

After the light disappeared, Sierra looked up. "That's it. "

"A whole lot easier than the ink and paper process," he said.

"And cleaner." Sierra chuckled. "Thanks for doing this and making my job easier."

Travis gave a sharp nod. "Anything else I can do?"

Sierra nibbled on her lip for a moment. "Since you asked, there are two blue bins in our van that I need."

"Give me your keys, and I'll grab them."

She dug the keys from her pocket. "Van's parked in the loading area out front."

She stood and stretched her back. "You can set the bins on the floor in the hallway outside this door. Don't want to contaminate the scene in here more than it's been with all the foot traffic today."

Claire's gut tightened. "If I'd known to cordon it off, I could have come up with some reason to keep people out."

"Would've been good, but what's done is done." Sierra flashed another one of her ready smiles.

Claire didn't buy this one though. What was done was done was the truth. Claire's software and the device had been stolen, and it was beginning to look like if she'd paid more attention to security that wouldn't have happened.

If that wasn't bad enough, because of the security issues, her life was also on the line, and the only way she could stay safe was to listen to the one man she'd never planned to see again.

6

Nearing four a.m., Travis met Gage at the institute's front door. Gage had traveled for over five hours, but didn't look any the worse for wear. He hadn't changed much since Travis had seen him last either.

Over six feet tall, wearing a black performance T-shirt and black tactical pants, he had dark hair he kept short. Still fit. Maybe more so. Perhaps from hours of PT for his arm or him bulking up elsewhere to compensate for the weakness in that arm.

Any way Travis looked at it, his buddy was a sight for sore eyes as Travis clapped him on the back. "Thanks for coming, man."

He waved a hand in front of his face. "I always forget the brutal humidity here in the summer."

"You'll want to drink lots of water."

"Thanks, Mom." He laughed. "You sound like I haven't been in worse weather than this and survived."

"Sorry. I haven't been able to do anything to help here so took the opportunity, I guess."

"Bad?"

Travis brought his buddy up to speed, including telling him about the Veritas partners and the security issues.

"You're lucky to get them on short notice," Gage said. "And to get them to fly across the country. Big score."

"All my colonel's doing. He can be very persuasive." One of the white-suited techs came out carrying evidence, and Travis stepped closer to Gage. "You have an IT person on your team, right?"

Gage's thick eyebrow rose. "I do, but you said Nick Thorn was here. He's tops in the field. You can't do any better than him. Even my person will tell you that."

"Except maybe we could find someone who's a little less intense."

Gage snorted. "Sounds like the pot calling the kettle black."

"Maybe, but he's got Claire feeling bad about security issues she'd trusted her staff to take care of."

Gage narrowed his eyes. "Claire, as in Dr. Reed, the program director?"

Travis nodded. "And before you go all Sherlock Holmes on me. Yeah, we had a thing back when we worked together. She broke it off."

"And you still have feelings for her."

"Yeah, maybe, but nothing's changed. She's still married to her job, and I'm tied to mine. Means we won't ever live in the same place."

"I get that, but take it from someone who lost the woman he loved." Gage locked gazes with Travis. "We aren't guaranteed a tomorrow, so don't make a stupid decision. Figure it out. If you want her, go after her."

Travis would honestly give Gage's comment some thought. Not now. Not when they were hunting her stalker. "I talked her into going home for a shower and to rest while

Veritas finishes their work. We could clear her rental house together then make a plan while she rests."

"Sounds good but it would help if I got a ten-cent tour of the place first so I know what we're dealing with here."

"Follow me." Travis swiped the temp card Claire had issued him through the wall-mounted reader and entered the research lab. Gage trailed him as he strode down the aisle to Claire's office, where she was sitting in front of her computer but staring into the distance as if lost in thought.

"I'd like you to meet my buddy, Gage Blackwell." Travis stepped out of the way so Gage could enter too.

He strode straight to the desk and held out his hand.

She shot to her feet and clasped his hand, her expression tight like an overtired and stressed individual. "Dr. Claire Reed, program director here. But call me Claire. Thank you for coming."

"Of course." Gage released her hand, and his gaze roved over the room. He had to be taking in every detail like he would've done on one of his former ops. "I only hope I can be of help."

She dropped back into her chair. "Travis told me all about your team in Oregon. Cold Harbor sounds like a lovely town."

"Off the beaten path for sure." Gage didn't show a hint of emotion. Why? Travis had no idea.

"Do you know the Veritas Center's partners?" she asked.

"I do. In fact, we have used them to process forensics in our investigations." Gage smiled. "Perhaps you could take me on a quick tour of the facility, and I can say hello along the way."

"Of course." Claire glanced at her computer, likely checking to be sure it had gone to sleep and locked itself while she'd been daydreaming. "Follow me."

She passed Travis and Gage on the way to the hall, and they trailed behind.

"She's a real stunner," Gage whispered to Travis. "And a doctor too. No wonder you fell for her."

Travis rolled his eyes.

Claire glanced over her shoulder at Gage. "I hope while you're in town, you'll be willing to run a few of our simulations."

"Sure thing. I mean, if you've been basing success on this guy's scores." Gage stabbed a finger in Travis's chest and grinned. "You don't know what success is."

"We'll see," Travis said, trying to keep his competitive spirit in check.

Claire laughed then continued on, handling the tour like a professional who'd conducted similar tours over the years, and she didn't show even a hint of that stress he'd seen in the office. She took Gage into the server room where Nick remained seated at the computer.

"Thorn," Gage said. "Heard you were being your usual prickly self, proving you're aptly named."

Claire cast a horrified look at Nick. "I didn't say anything."

"It was me," Travis admitted.

"Well, you were right." Nick gave Claire a sheepish look. "I get on my high horse when things aren't done the way I would do them. If I promise to be on my best behavior for the rest of my time here, I hope you'll forget it ever happened."

She waved a hand. "It's already forgotten."

"But not the things I want you to fix, right? I mean because—"

"There you go again, Thorn." Gage shook his head.

"Sorry." He grinned. "Probably would be best if you moved on."

Claire laughed.

"Good thing you're also charming," Gage said.

Nick rubbed the back of his hand over his shirt and smiled. "That I am."

Gage rolled his eyes and looked at Claire. "Please save me from more of this."

"Just a second," Nick said, his tone sharp and alert now. "Before you go, you'll want to know I'm on your thief's trail. He tried to hide, but he didn't count on the server backup that was in process and didn't modify those files. So I found him. Just like I said I would."

"But who *is* he?" Claire asked, her good humor gone.

Nick frowned. "That I can't answer yet and might never be able to, but I can and will tell you exactly what he did when he invaded the network."

"Thank you." Claire's expression was unreadable, and Travis wanted to know what she was thinking.

"Okay," Nick said, his attention going back to the computer. "That's all for now."

She looked at Gage and Travis. "Follow me."

Travis had loved seeing her lighter side before the stress set in again. Seeing the woman he'd fallen in love with. Of course, she wasn't smiling and laughing because of him or even for him. Still, he'd enjoyed her good mood while it lasted.

They continued the tour and found Sierra working with her team in the equipment room. Squatting on the floor near the empty cubby, she had tweezers and an evidence bag in her hands. She used the tweezers to pick something up and deposited it into the bag, then stood and caught sight of them.

"Hey, Gage." She flashed him one of her earnest smiles that Travis was coming to associate with her. "Didn't expect to see you in Florida."

"We go way back." Gage clapped Travis on the back. "When he sends up the Bat signal I come running."

Claire rolled her eyes and looked at Sierra. "Did you find something?"

Sierra held out the bag. "A crushed seashell."

"Oh, that." Claire let out a long breath of disappointment. "Could've come from anywhere or anyone. Crushed shells are commonly used in place of gravel here."

"True." Sierra closed the bag. "But we can still analyze the shell, and if you find a strong suspect, perhaps we can tie it to their landscape. Worse case, we can find out what type of shell it is and locate the companies in the area who supply these shells. Then maybe find a purchase record of such shells from your suspect."

"Oh, wow." Claire blinked a few times. "That's great."

Was it? To Travis that sounded like days of work which would only help *once* they found the suspect. He'd hoped for something that could give them a suspect's identity tonight.

Sierra dropped the bag into a bin marked *Evidence*. "When does your cleaning crew come in to empty your trash?"

"We have a full-time janitor. He cleans and empties trash throughout the day."

Sierra pursed her lips. "Does every can get emptied every day?"

"For the most part, yes. But there are exceptions. If a room is in use during his scheduled rounds he'll skip it."

"Do you know when this room is cleaned?" Sierra held out her hands.

"Usually the last thing in the day after we're finished using the equipment."

"What are you getting at here?" Travis asked, losing patience.

"If trash was emptied at the end of the day, and your

suspect was the one who disabled the security at eleven, he could've been the first person to deposit trash in the bottom of the bag."

"Oh, yeah," Claire said. "I suppose so."

"And that's important because?" Travis asked, trying to remain patient.

"Because..." Sierra reached into her evidence bin to pull out two bags. "I recovered a bloody tissue and Band-Aid wrappers in the bottom of the trash in here. Not a lot of blood, but I also recovered more from a sharp screw on the cubby where your missing device was stored."

Claire's eyes brightened. "That's good news! You could have our suspect's DNA."

"Possible." Sierra's tone was more reserved than Claire's expression. "We can analyze the tissue as well. If it's a brand name, we can likely narrow it down to the manufacturer, so if you have staff who keep tissues on their desk, we can compare."

"If they took the tissue from their own desk," Gage said.

"Good point," Sierra said. "We'll also be sure to process your first aid kit in case the Band-Aid was taken from there. We should have good DNA recovery there and in here."

"But what can you tell us from the DNA?" Claire asked.

"Unfortunately, not much right now. If you'd collected DNA on all of your employees, which I doubt, to use as comparison, we run our samples against it. Without that, we won't have anything to match our results to and the DNA will come into play at the trial."

"No DNA on file, and I can't very well go around asking for samples." A heavy sigh slipped from Claire's lips.

"Once you identify a likely suspect, we *can* collect one easy enough. However, we would need to recover it in a manner that would hold up in a court of law." She returned the bags to the box. "We can talk about that if it becomes necessary."

"But you can run it against CODIS," Gage said.

"The FBI's DNA database," Sierra stated. "Yes, we can and will in case we're looking at an outsider who might have a criminal record."

Claire tapped her chin. "I have to wonder if this might eliminate the people who access the device most often."

"How's that?" Sierra asked.

"We all know about that sharp screw because at one time or another we've cut ourselves on it. So we avoid it. But someone not familiar with the cubby might not."

"Possible or could be the person was just in a hurry or nervous and forgot," Gage said.

"What about blood types?" Travis asked, grasping at anything that might help. "Can you type the blood, and if it's rare, might we be able to ID someone that way?"

"You could narrow things down that way and then get a DNA sample."

"But you'd have to ask people their blood types," Gage weighed in.

"I could do that." Claire's voice raised. "Maybe I could pretend the subject of how many people knew their blood type came up in conversation, and I was taking a poll to see who did know it."

"Sounds like that might work," Sierra said.

"You'd have to be careful not to raise any suspicions," Travis warned.

"I can handle it." Claire lifted her chin and eyed him.

She was issuing him a challenge. He loved when she did that. When she stood up to him. When it wasn't dangerous, that was. And this could be if she approached people the wrong way.

"Tell you what," Sierra said. "I'll go ahead and get you

that information the minute I return to the lab. That way if the blood type is unique and you decide to do it, you'll have the info."

"Which will be when?" Travis asked.

"We've got a few more hours here, then we'll have to clean up to remove all evidence of our visit and catch our flight." She looked around the room. "That's going to be so different for us. We never clean up the fingerprint powder, but it could be a good thing for us to see how the other side handles things."

Travis liked her positive take on the subject. Seemed to him that she was a positive person altogether. It was good for them to have her here when they weren't locating many leads.

"We can help with the cleaning," Claire said.

"I'd appreciate that. Now I need to get back to work." Sierra smiled at Gage. "Good to see you again, Gage."

He nodded and returned the smile with a reserved one.

Claire stepped into the hallway. "Let's wrap this tour up. I'd like to get that shower in and come back here in plenty of time to help clean."

She was true to her word and finished the tour quickly, until Nick poked his head out of the server room to stop them.

"I've tracked your intruder." Nick dropped into the chair. "He waltzed in and downloaded the software to an external drive from this computer."

"So like downloading something from the internet then?" Travis asked.

"Not quite that simple. First, there are security measures in place to prevent use of any external devices on this computer, and he had to bypass that. Then the software had security measures too that he had to get around. But he did." Nick leaned his chair back and clasped his hands behind his head. "And I have to say, I'm impressed with his skills. Efficient and creative."

"We haven't really determined that we're looking for a *he*," Claire said. "True, my attacker was male, but he could be working for a woman."

"Right, I was using he as hackers are more often male than female." He grabbed the sticky note she'd given him with the login and jotted something on it. "This is the login used to access the network at eleven-fourteen p.m. yesterday."

"Wait, what?" Claire gaped at him. "That's the person who stole the software?"

He held out the note. "It is indeed. Your thief's identity in writing."

7

Travis reached out for the sticky note, but Claire snatched the paper from Nick's hand first. Travis looked over her shoulder as she stared at the information. Not a name as Travis had hoped, but a login that didn't give a clue as to the person's identity.

She looked at Nick. "This doesn't give even a hint of who accessed the network, but I can at least find it on our login list."

"Already did." Nick grinned. "The network login is registered to a former employee, Mike Robb."

"Mike? No." She shook her head hard. "Not possible. I personally deactivated his key card and network credentials."

"He's on your suspect list," Travis pointed out.

Her posture stiffened. "Yes, but I honestly didn't believe it could be him. I mean how would he have reactivated his credentials?"

Gage moved closer. "Who has authority to activate and issue key cards and network logins?"

"Me and our security manager, Warren White." She

clasped a hand at her chest. "I surely didn't do it and couldn't imagine Warren doing it either."

"No need to speculate on this." Nick swiveled back to the computer. "As I said, I can track the changes, and I'll let you know who reactivated the credentials. Assuming the person didn't hide their trail."

She continued to eye Nick. "Have you looked at the internal security logs to see if a key card was used to gain access to this room?"

Nick glanced over his shoulder. "No one swiped a card after seven p.m. until seven-thirty-two am for any room in the building. Not helpful, I know, but I'll include the log in my report so you have it and can see the last and first people to use cards. I'm going to look for cameras next. Maybe we have some video to go on, though as meticulously as this theft seems to be planned, I'm going to assume the cameras were disabled too."

"Thanks, Nick."

"And might I add, we should be looking into this security manager. He has the ability to make the changes that made this theft possible."

"But I told you," Claire said, not hiding her irritation. "Warren's out of town at a conference this week."

"He could be working with someone who took the device, but he stole the software," Gage said. "Can he access the network remotely?"

Claire shook her head. "In fact, he insisted on not allowing remote access. The risk would be too great. We don't allow employees to work from home, and we don't have workers who travel for the job, so it's not necessary."

"A real solid decision." Nick smiled at her, offering the first praise Travis could recall.

"Glad we finally did something right," she said.

"Hey," Nick said. "Your security isn't bad. Could just be

improved."

"Couldn't this White fella tell Claire he's not allowing remote access then access it from outside the building anyway?" Gage asked.

"He could, but I checked it out," Nick said. "No one has accessed the server remotely." "I'll get a full report to you, including all access records and log files by end of day tomorrow."

"Thanks, Nick." Claire spun and charged into the hallway. "I just need to grab my purse, and I'm ready to go home for that shower. I'll meet you at the door."

She rushed away as if running from Travis. Or did she just need some time alone, even if it was only a few minutes to get her purse? Travis could see that. He'd pretty much been glued to her side since he'd arrived, except for his time in the training session.

Travis walked with Gage toward the exit.

Gage scowled. "Not a lot to go on to find our thief."

"I was thinking the same thing." Travis tried not to sound dejected.

"It's looking like it'll be harder to find an insider because they know how to hide their tracks. But after seeing the place, I have to say the odds are good that it's someone who works here. Getting past guards and on campus makes it nearly impossible for an outsider to pull this off."

"I don't know." Travis eyed Gage. "We could both be on campus in the blink of an eye and you know it."

"But we're highly trained to breach target locations, and I can't see any spec ops guy or former spec ops guy wanting to steal and sell a program designed to help train recruits."

"You're right. But I still think we should keep our options open. That's why I've already asked my colonel to get the log book and security feed for the front gate for the time of the theft. See who, if anyone, came on campus."

Gage shook his head. "Well, why didn't you say so?"

"Because I still think it's a long shot."

"How many times did long shots pay off on a mission in-country?"

Too many to count. And too many to be comfortable with because if they had reached the point of needing a long shot, then their plan had been ripped apart and no longer worked for them. Which was when they had to think on their feet, and as the leader on most missions, the team looked to Travis for answers.

"We need to do a deep dive on Mike Robb." Travis told Gage about his personal connection to Claire. "With Nick tied up with the network, can you get your IT person to do it? Maybe include a check on Warren White too, but let's keep that one quiet for now."

Gage arched a dark brow. "You mean don't tell Claire?"

Travis nodded.

"Your call, but it could come back to bite you." Gage got out his phone.

"I figured you'd wait until morning to call."

"Why? My staff knows to be ready on a moment's notice. Plus, Eryn's a night owl." He tapped the screen. "Eryn, good. I need a deep dive on a Mike Robb and Warren White out of Orlando. I'll text you their particulars. Need it yesterday."

Travis heard a female voice on the line but not what she said before Gage ended the call.

Claire marched down the hallway, swinging her purse, her step lighter. Maybe she'd learned something. Or maybe she was pinning all of her hopes on the Mike Robb lead, which Travis thought wasn't much of a lead at all. Although Nick proved the time of the intrusion by Robb, more likely someone else reissued the card in Robb's name, but he had nothing to do with it.

"We need Mike Robb's address and phone number so

Gage's IT person can do a deep dive on him," he said, thinking about how they might get Warren White's particulars. Likely Eryn could find him without their help.

"Hold on." She dug in her purse for her key card and then swiped it over the nearest door. Travis grabbed it before it closed so he could keep an eye on her. She went to the nearest computer and logged in then called out Robb's personal information.

Gage typed the data into his phone. So did Travis. He was going to pay the guy a visit tomorrow. Nothing they learned tonight would stop that.

She logged off the computer and pushed past Travis to start for the door. "Let's get a move on, so we can be back here in time to help."

"Hold up." Travis stepped in front of her. "We need to clear the area and bring the car to the curb to minimize any danger to you."

She peered at him, eyes darkening. "Is that really necessary?"

"I'll make a sweep and get my car," Gage said before Travis could answer.

Travis figured his buddy didn't want to stand around and argue when action could be taken.

"I know you want to find the missing prototype," Travis said. "But if I haven't made it clear, let me do so now. Your safety comes above everything. Everything."

She took a step back. Maybe from his forceful tone. He shouldn't have scared her, but she needed to take her safety seriously. He plunged on before she could argue.

"To that end, whenever you leave or enter a building, Gage and I will be with you. One of us checking things out, the other at your side."

"Okay," she said.

"I know you're used to thinking for yourself. Making

snap decisions. But during those transit times, more than any other time, we'll do the thinking for you, and we need you to listen to our directives. No second-guessing our commands or refusing to comply."

"Got it," she said tersely.

"And don't get mad at me for having to be such a dictator. We can kiss and make up when I get you to your place without incident." He grinned but kept his gaze roving for Gage.

She didn't smile, but her shoulders relaxed a notch.

Gage pulled up and got out to open the back door of his large SUV. "We're clear to move."

"Straight into the car." Travis took her arm and led her out the door to rush her into the vehicle. He climbed in beside her.

Gage closed the door and ran around the front to the driver's seat to get them heading toward the exit. He stopped at the guard booth.

Claire lowered her window, letting in a wet wash of sultry air. She smiled at the young officer on guard duty.

He stepped forward and cast a suspicious look at Gage and Travis. "Everything okay, Dr. Reed?"

"Everything's fine. Lieutenant Chapman and Mr. Blackwell will be spending a few days working here with me. We're leaving for a bit, but will be back in an hour or so."

He cocked his head. "And your other guests?"

"Still working."

"Roger that." He saluted Claire and opened the gate.

Gage pulled through, and Claire gave him her home address, which he plugged into GPS.

They rode in silence to her rental house. Not a comfortable silence, but one that spoke to the danger of the situation and the unease Claire continued to have with Travis. Shoot, he was uneasy too. Gage seemed to pick up on it as he kept moving in the front seat as if squirming under the tension and wanting to get out. Travis didn't blame his buddy. He was taught to notice personal dynamics and couldn't be missing the tension.

Gage pulled into the driveway of the house Claire had moved to since she'd given Travis his marching orders. Outside security lights came on, and he got a good look at the stucco bungalow painted white with black windows and trim and boasting a clay roof.

"I've got the outside," Gage said and climbed out.

Claire faced Travis. "Seems like the two of you are in sync."

"We worked quite a few missions together, and you learn to predict what the other person needs before they ask."

"I watched your training video. Got a feel for what you must go through on your ops." She bit her lip. "It was at the same time scary and impressive."

"I really did good, didn't I?" He started to grin, but Gage approached and signaled that the house was clear, and all good humor evaporated.

"Get your keys out for Gage so he can open the door."

She fished them from her purse and handed them out the window. "You'll need my security code too." She shared it with him.

He marched to the door, got it open, and light flooded out into the night, but he entered instead of signaling to them.

"He's clearing the inside, and we should be able to go in soon."

She bobbed her knee until Gage stepped to the end of the walkway and waved them in. Then she sat up straight, her eyes wide.

"Wait for me to get to your door, then straight to the entrance, past Gage, and he'll bring up the rear."

She hopped out, and Travis tucked her under his arm to usher her into her house. The aromatic eucalyptus wreath on the front door caught his attention. Too bad the medicinal scent did nothing to diminish the sour taste lingering in his mouth over her continued unease around him. Nor did it do anything to lighten the agitation he felt in her presence. That never left his mind when he wasn't busy worrying about her safety.

Gage closed the door and locked it.

Travis followed her to a room with contemporary furniture in neutral colors, but his attention went straight to a wall-to-wall glass door overlooking her backyard. The lawn backed to a natural green space with brush and trees tangled into a thick jungle where Claire's abductor could take cover. The unobstructed view of the space was nice. Great, in fact. *If* you weren't trying to defend the place. A fence would've been better. Not that he believed the man who risked attacking Claire in broad daylight would let a fence stand in his way. And that meant Travis needed to keep his focus on his job.

He faced Claire. "I'd like to inspect your security measures."

"Security measures?" She laughed. "This is a house not a military base."

"Let me check your locks, then," he said before he let that smile take him back in time, and he sent his buddy packing and did something he would regret.

She held out her hands. "Help yourself."

"To start, I'll be bunking on the couch tonight."

"I think you'd be more comfortable in my guest room."

"My assignment isn't about comfort. The couch is next to the patio door, which my initial impression says is your most vulnerable point of entry. Any intruder would have to get past me to reach your bedroom."

She shivered and wrapped her arms around her waist, her gaze darting around the room as if it no longer felt like a safe haven.

He hated that he'd worried her and despite his self-preservation warning him to stay away, he rested a hand on her shoulder.

Surprisingly, she didn't back away.

"I'll do everything in my power to ensure that no one hurts you, Claire."

"Thank you." A sincere smile crossed her lips, lighting her face and firing his pulse.

A slideshow of the playful, loving woman he'd fallen for started rolling through his mind. Her laughter. Her joy. All of it reminded him that this lighthearted woman still existed —just not for him. He swallowed hard and forced his mind back to the job.

He jerked a thumb at Gage. "Besides this old guy needs a real bed now. He's not used to roughing it anymore."

"Funny." Gage rolled his eyes. "I'll just toddle off to my car for our bags."

Travis laughed. "And I'll check out those locks."

Ignoring Claire's continued focus on him, he went down a small hallway. Things were happening so fast between them, and he didn't know what to make of it. Only a few hours together and he felt like raising the white flag of surrender and finding a way out of the op. But he wasn't a quitter.

He called on years of training to focus and carefully evaluated two modestly sized bedrooms before stepping back through the family room to the master. He could feel Claire's eyes tracking him, and he wished she'd find some-thing—anything—else to do, but she trailed him as he checked every nook and cranny of the house.

"Everything good?" she asked, still watching him.

Good? No. Far from it. "Where's your safe room?"

"My what?" She pushed up her glasses.

"Where you take shelter from tornadoes." With few basements in a city boasting volatile summer weather, most residents had designated an internal room for shelter.

"Oh, that. The laundry room, why?"

"I want to establish a place for you to go in the event of an intrusion. I also suggest you sleep in your clothes in case we need to use the room or flee the house."

"Okay." That fear crept back into her eyes, making her seem vulnerable and alone.

He forced himself to turn away. "Show me the room."

She led the way to a room, if you could call it that. The space was barely bigger than the appliances. He made a quick assessment and then looked straight at her, making sure his expression conveyed the importance of his upcoming directions. "If I'm somehow disabled or if I tell you to come here, you head to this room and lock the door. No questions asked. No dallying. Straight in here. Got it?"

She gave a certain nod, but the fear lingered.

"We'll pick up a deadbolt and secure this space." Hoping to eliminate the heavy tension between them before he exploded, he grinned. "Don't worry. I'll repair any damage my bumbling skills cause before I leave town."

A wobbly smile lifted one side of her mouth, and though he wanted to give her additional safety instructions, he thought it best to pass the advice on in small snippets before she totally freaked out.

He jerked a thumb over his shoulder. "Go ahead and grab that shower then I'll take one after you're done."

Travis returned to the family room as Gage entered again.

"I'll take those keys." Travis held out his hand. "I'm going to take a look outside."

Gage widened his stance. "You don't trust my recon skills."

"I do. I just want to get the lay of the land."

"This really has you freaked."

Travis held up his hand. "Before you say that I'm overreacting, can you think of one good reason I should relax?"

"No," Gage said. "No, I can't."

"Exactly." Travis headed for the door.

He stepped out into the evening air, forgetting how high the humidity levels could be in Orlando. He'd once thought he would ask Claire to marry him, but to be together, one of them would have to quit their job and move to another state. If he was being honest, he was thinking she would make the move as he didn't really want to live in such stifling weather. Nor did he want to leave the team.

Plus, Claire was far more employable than he was. What kind of job could he find?

Didn't matter now, did it?

He shook it off and moved around the house. High shrubs in the front gave plenty of hiding spaces to a would-be attacker. Too late to trim them back. He would just have to be sure they made a thorough check behind each shrub each time they returned.

He eased around the side and down a slight incline to the gate. He reached over to open it and entered the back-yard that the large patio door faced. The space was wide open and lit by landscape lights that illuminated a large deck and lush tropical plants ringing the perimeter.

Beautiful. Peaceful even. But additional places for that potential attacker to hide.

Loud pounding sounded on the glass door from the inside.

Travis's heart rate kicked up, and he spun.

Gage opened a section of the bi-fold door. "We have a situation here."

Stomach knotting, Travis charged across the deck and inside.

Dressed in conservative black pants and a white blouse, Claire stood in the family room, her hair wet. Her eyes were narrowed, and she clutched her phone tightly in her hand.

"What is it?" he asked, dreading her answer.

She lifted her phone. "A call. I got a call. It was the person who stole the prototype."

Anger roared through Travis, but he swallowed to keep it in check and not scare Claire even more. "Did you recognize the voice?"

She shrugged. "Maybe. It was distorted. You know like you hear on those TV shows. So I couldn't identify the voice but the cadence was familiar."

"Cadence?" he asked.

"A distinct pausing after certain words was familiar." She shuddered and clasped her arms around her waist.

It took everything he was made of to stand there instead of sweeping her into his arms. He had to look away from her, but his imagination flared, seeing her on the phone with this guy.

Unacceptable.

He gritted his teeth and tried to radiate calm. "And who does this cadence resemble?"

"Mike. Mike Robb."

Travis sucked in a sharp breath. "Your stalker."

"Maybe stalker."

Travis didn't care about that little detail. As far as Travis was concerned, the guy was a stalker, and he would be talking to Mike Robb as soon as he could get eyes on him.

8

Nearing eight a.m. and the arrival of staff, Claire scrubbed her fingernails in the restroom down the hall from her office. The black fingerprint powder left her hands and circled the drain. Was she really cleaning away the gritty powder or the very thought that someone had invaded her office? Her sanctuary away from home? Not that it would ever be that again.

"Focus, Claire," she said to the mirror, ignoring the residual fear in her reflection. "Keep your mind on the job, and that's how the guy will be caught."

She turned off the water, dried her hands on brown paper towels, then headed for her office where Gage and Travis were going to meet her after they washed up too. Cleanup had gone well, but the insidious black fingerprint powder had permeated every area it touched. Still, Sierra was as meticulous in cleaning as she was in making the mess. Hopefully, they'd done a thorough enough job so no questions were asked.

And she also hoped their network manager didn't see Nick's adventures recorded in the logs. Nick said he didn't have time to hide his work, but he did disable the report that would normally have been sent to their manager notifying him of after-hours network access. If he discovered Nick's work, she'd gotten permission from Colonel Vogler to tell him about the theft.

She entered her office, where Gage straddled a chair, and Travis sat on the corner of her desk. She held up her hands. "Sorry. Took longer than I thought to get clean."

"No worries." Travis smiled at her. "Gave us time to review the security log books from the front gates."

"Locate anything?"

He shook his head. "So we should get to planning our investigative steps for today."

"Don't forget that I'm going to be testing that simulation software to take over the top slot." Gage smirked at Travis.

"Like that'll happen." Travis rolled his eyes and then focused on Claire.

She sat behind her desk. "I guess one of the first things that needs to happen is we need to talk to Mike."

"Not we." Travis came to his feet. "*I'll* talk to him while you remain here with Gage."

She tried to hide her frustration as Travis was only doing what he thought best for her. "He's not going to hurt me."

"You can't know that," Gage said. "Not if he's the guy who tried to abduct you."

"I just don't see him doing that."

"I do." Travis planted his feet. "Having worked here, he knows the value of the software. He knows where the device is stored and what it takes to get to it. He knows that no one can access the software without you. A reason to abduct you, and if not for that, he's stalking you. So he's the most logical suspect."

"I hear you, I really do, I just don't think he would do it."

"Then I'll have to prove it to you." Travis gritted his teeth.

"Is there any scenario where you *would* believe this is an inside job?" Gage asked.

She crossed her arms. "I know it looks like that's what happened, but I trust my staff."

She was far too trusting. Always had been. The exact opposite of Travis, but then she supposed he learned not to trust others on the job as a way to stay alive.

"Just keep an open mind, okay?" he asked.

"I'll do my best," she said and meant it.

"Any ideas where I can find Robb?"

She leaned back to think. "He's really a frugal guy but loves seafood. He always used to go to a local place for the shrimp specials on Wednesdays."

"And today is Wednesday," Travis said.

Gage's phone rang, and he looked at the screen. "Text from Eryn. She's emailing Robb's background report. She said page three is interesting." Gage thumbed through his phone and looked at Claire. "I'm assuming I can't access your printers so give me your email, and I'll forward this to be printed."

Claire shared her email address, and then opened her laptop to wait for the report, her mind already spinning over what page three might hold.

"Got it," she said.

"Print a copy for each of us," Travis said.

She sent it to the printer, but scanned down to page three while the printer whirred into action. The report declared that Mike had a restraining order issued by his former wife.

Travis grabbed the reports and handed them out.

"His ex-wife had a restraining order issued for him," Claire said.

Travis raised an eyebrow. "Further evidence that he has stalker tendencies."

Claire didn't really want to believe that, but she was starting to. "I wonder how he passed his background check with something like that on his record."

"Eryn's good at her job, and she can find things many others miss," Gage said. "Plus, archive records are being put online all the time by law enforcement. Maybe it was added after his hire."

"Either way, he's the man we need to start with." Travis eyed Claire. "So this leaves Robb firmly as a suspect along with Norton, who we need to start investigating too."

"I'll text Eryn to do a deep dive on Norton." Gage got out his phone and started typing.

"You were going to review other staff to include women too," Travis said. "Anyone come to mind?"

Claire hated to add more of her dedicated workers to the list, but she had to do this. "Ruth Sadler and Bethany Jennings are the most obvious. I heard Ruth say she was one step away from getting evicted for not being able to pay the increase in her rent. She's a software developer, so she could have the skills to disable the systems."

"And Bethany?" Gage asked.

Claire took a breath. "She's less likely. She's our receptionist and as far as I know doesn't have the skills to pull this off. But she does have knowledge of how things work around here and that might make partnering with someone on the theft a possibility."

"Why do you think she might have done it?" Travis asked.

"She always has the latest designer handbags and shoes. She can't possibly afford them on her admin salary. She says they're knockoffs, but I've heard others say she's lying."

"So you think they both need money," Gage said.

Claire nodded. "I can talk to them to see if they have an alibi for the night of the theft. Not sure how I'll broach the subject, but I'll figure it out. Doesn't matter for the time of the attack though. Neither of them could be my attacker."

Travis looked at his watch. "You could question them while Gage and I run testing scenarios before lunch. Then I'll head out to talk to Robb."

"Okay," she said, but the thought of Travis leaving left a hitch in her chest.

In less than twenty-four hours, she'd come to depend on him for her safety. A legit thing she supposed, given her situation, and something she could deal with as the need for his protection was temporary.

Just as long as she didn't start to count on him for anything else. Could she spend time with him and avoid that? She had to.

Her phone chimed with a text. She glanced at the screen. "It's from Sierra. The blood type from the sample is O positive."

"The most common type and won't likely help us narrow things down," Gage said.

Travis nodded. "It was a long shot anyway."

"Yeah, but I had my hopes up." Frowning, Claire took the men to Julie to arrange testing, then went to find Bethany at the front desk.

Claire dug deep for as genuine of a smile as she could find. "Good morning, Bethany."

The petite redhead smiled at Claire. "Going to be another hot one. Will you go running again or is it too hot for you?"

Was she just making small talk or planning another abduction? "Too hot."

"I figured as much. And then there was the attack. That would put me off running for sure."

"It was terrifying." Claire hoped this could be her way in.

"You haven't had anyone strange try to get in here, have you? Or anyone asking questions about me?"

She shook her head, hair scraped back in a bun holding firm. "I'd have told you and the police if I had."

"I figured as much, but just had to ask." *And I have to lie to get info on your whereabouts.* "I went running Monday night after it got cooler. It was late. Around eleven. I got the feeling I wasn't alone. Do you live close to here? Maybe saw something that night?"

"I live close, but not really close enough to see anything. Besides, Monday is my painting class, and we go until all hours of the night. That night I was really engrossed in the subject and didn't get home until two a.m." She tapped a long purple fingernail on the desk. "We're painting a semi-nude male. It's hard to stop looking at that." She grinned.

"I can imagine." Claire cast her a dug-up smile. "Let me know if anyone odd comes in, okay? I'm on edge until the police catch this guy."

"Oh, I hear you. I've started having someone walk me to my car at night."

"Good plan. I hope others are doing the same thing."

"Not all of us have two hunky spec ops guys hanging around." She winked at Claire.

Claire faked a laugh and stepped away to go in search of Ruth. The team's only software developer, she had a small cubicle in the back of the IT department. She sat at her desk, head down, concentrating on her work. She was a shy woman and working alone suited her. Sure, she was a part of the team, but she didn't have to interact with them to do her daily tasks.

"Hey, Ruth." Claire leaned on the top of the low cubicle wall.

She batted her lashes and released her mouse. "What are you doing here? Did I do something wrong?"

Just like Ruth to think she was in trouble. "Nothing wrong at all. Your work is always exemplary."

Her face reddened. "So how can I help you?"

"I heard you mention that your rent had gone up a lot."

"Oh, right. Yeah, I was complaining. Sorry."

"No need to be sorry. I was just wondering where you live. I have a friend looking, and I want to make sure not to have your complex on my list." Another lie and she hated it just as much as the first.

"Don't get me wrong, it's a nice complex if they can afford it, but it's going up to two grand a month for one bedroom. That's a twenty-five percent increase." She shared the complex name.

Claire didn't recognize it, but it really wasn't important. "That would be in their price range. Is it quiet?"

"Yeah. Real quiet."

"No loud parties or noisy neighbors to keep you up at night?"

"Occasionally on the weekend but never during the week. But I'm a night owl so..."

"A night owl? Maybe you saw the moon Monday night? I was out running around eleven. Fabulous." She hoped it had been fabulous as she was sound asleep and had no idea.

"I'm not much on the outdoors. Was hunkered down in my gaming cave with my online friends like I do most nights."

"Sounds like fun." Claire smiled. "Okay, thanks for the info on your complex."

She left Ruth behind to head to the training facility. Both Ruth and Bethany had an alibi that could be checked out if needed. But just like Hector, there was no way Claire could follow up without raising suspicions, which she didn't want to do. So for now she would trust these three weren't lying and focus on Mike and Kent. Unless, of course, Travis or Gage had a different take on things.

She joined Julie in the observation room. Gage was running a mountain scenario and Travis leaned against the wall, his ankles crossed in a lazy pose, but his gaze was intense and focused as usual.

Claire was interested in the progress, but even if she was consumed by the theft right now, Julie would expect Claire to be involved in this testing. "How's it going?"

"Good. Travis killed this scenario. Gage is just a bit off. He seems to baby his right arm."

Claire nodded. "An arm injury sustained in an accident. His reason for leaving the SEALS."

"Ah, that explains it. But look at his scores." She stood back from the main computer. "He's still more impressive than anyone else who's run the test. Anyone except Travis."

Claire studied the screen, confirming Julie's take on the situation.

The scenario ended, and Gage took off his virtual device. He rolled his right shoulder and looked at his arm. "I'd be smoking you if only this stupid thing worked right."

"I'm sorry about the accident," Travis said.

Claire was afraid the guys might forget about Julie and start talking about the theft. She muted the mic for a moment and turned to Julie. "No point in us both staying here. I can finish up."

"Okay." Julie marched from the room but she looked a bit frustrated. She was never fond of doing grunt work, which is likely what she had waiting for her, but it was in her job description, and Claire tried to do her share of it too.

Claire felt bad for the abrupt end of her conversation and wished she could tell Julie what was going on. But Claire had no choice but to send Julie away. She couldn't be party to any discussion the guys might have about the theft. With her assistant gone, Claire turned the mic on.

Gage waved a hand. "No need to be sorry about the accident. Was all my fault. Alcohol and motorcycles don't mix."

"But the alcohol and joyride were a result of losing your wife."

"True that, but I chose to act out. I could've trusted God and got on with my life in a proper way. So as much as I hate this injury..." He flexed his arm again. "I caused it and now I live with it the best I can."

"By forming a team of former military or law enforcement people just like you."

Gage nodded. "God's way of making something good from bad. A second chance for all of us, really."

"And from what Jackson says, you built a compound most spec ops guys would be envious of."

Gage grinned. "I might've gone a little overboard."

Travis smiled. "I have to get out there and see it."

"You're welcome any time." Gage's phone rang, and he got it out. "Eryn. Putting you on speaker so Travis can hear."

"Hey, Travis." Eryn's pleasant voice came over the speaker. "Nice to meet you. Gage speaks very highly of you."

"Ditto," Travis said.

"Maybe you could come out to Oregon when all of this is over and those of us who aren't sunning ourselves in Orlando can meet you in person."

"No sunning going on here," Gage said.

"Hmm, right." She laughed. "If you come back with a tan we'll all know the truth."

"Hey, I arrived with a tan so you can't measure that." Gage chuckled. "You have something to tell me?"

"Boy, do I." Her excited tone had Claire leaning closer to the speaker. "I finished my report on Warren White. The guy is not who he says he is. Figured I should call on this one before I send it."

What? Not who he says he is? What did that mean? Claire needed to know.

"Okay, now you've got my interest," Gage said.

"What do you mean not who he says he is?" Travis demanded.

Claire appreciated him demanding the answer she wanted too.

"Just what it sounds like. His real name is Fitz Ellwood. He assumed Warren White's identity in 1997 when White died."

Claire had to be in on this discussion. She ran out the door and into the room with the men. "How can that be? Everyone goes through a deep background check before we hire."

"Eryn, meet Claire Reed."

"Oh, sorry," Claire said. "Sorry to barge into your call, but I have to know what's going on in my own team."

"No worries," Eryn said. "I'd want to know too."

"Give us the details," Gage said.

"White and Ellwood were college roommates. They actually became friends because they looked so much alike and people were mistaking them. The real Warren White died in a boating accident. Ellwood was drunk and piloting the boat. White had no family so Ellwood assumed White's identity to escape a potential manslaughter charge. By the time the police recovered the body, he was decomposed enough that the only ID they could make was from what they found in his pocket and from Ellwood's confirmation of what White was wearing."

"What about DNA?" Gage asked. "Didn't they run it for ID?"

"No," Eryn said firmly. "The real Ellwood reported the

boating accident pretending to be White. He claimed Ellwood was driving and White was washed overboard. Then said that Ellwood jumped in to try to save him, but he got a cramp and disappeared underwater. White couldn't save him. So the police didn't think there was any foul play and didn't run DNA."

Claire stared at the phone. "But how did you find this out when our government background check failed?"

"First, they had no reason to think he was lying about his name, so they only investigated Warren White."

"But what about fingerprints?" Travis asked.

"Not a problem. Neither men had been printed before so Ellwood's prints became the first ones registered for White and checked out as having a clear record. They both had the same degrees and worked similar jobs, but Ellwood quit White's job right away so he wasn't found out by the people he worked with. It's been clear sailing since then."

"Okay, so the prints checked out fine," Travis said. "But how did you learn about it?"

"The secrets of the dark web," Eryn said, her tone holding a smile. "Apparently, he's a Boy Scout leader, and his picture was included in an Orlando newspaper article. A hacker, Ross Garland, saw it and recognized him as Ellwood. Garland went to college with Ellwood and White for a year, but flunked out. Blamed Ellwood for some of his problems. Garland found Ellwood in a chat room on the dark web, bad-mouthing Ellwood and threatening to go public unless Ellwood paid up."

"Did he?" Claire held her breath in wait for the answer.

"Not sure on that, but I am sure that Garland was murdered the same week, and the murder remains unsolved."

Claire gasped. "Warren. You think Warren did this?"

"Could be."

"But the police don't know about White or Ellwood or whatever we want to call him?" Gage asked.

"No, which is not unusual as the dark web is a whole different animal to navigate and local police don't usually have access. And the background check was done long before this murder or dark web chat happened."

Claire could hardly believe all of this. A man she worked with day in and day out wasn't who he said he was. What else might he be hiding? "What about Fitz Ellwood's family? Didn't they report him missing?"

"No," Eryn said. "They were estranged from him."

"We need to call the police," Claire said.

"We can't without telling them why we're looking into White to begin with," Gage said.

Travis looked between her and Gage. "I suggest we keep this info to ourselves until I contact my CO and read him in."

"But this dark web business says he could be our guy, right?" Claire asked.

"I'm not ready to go there," Eryn said. "There's no trail of him trying to sell the prototype and software on the dark web. Or engage in any other nefarious activities. And my other checks say he's a real Boy Scout. Literally and figuratively. Leads a squeaky-clean life. Like he's taking advantage of having changed his background."

Interesting. "Then why was he on the dark web at all?"

"He was posing as a hacker, trying to gain info on network intrusion techniques. I think he was doing it to discover how better to defend against attacks on your network."

"Boy Scout or not, we'll be looking into him more," Travis said. "But for now, we hold off reporting him until I get permission from my CO to read the police in."

"Agreed," Gage said.

"Me too." Claire didn't want Warren to get away with stealing his friend's identity for another hour, but it was the best thing to do right now.

The moment Colonel Vogler gave them the green light, she would be on the phone to Detective Purcell and Warren White or Fitz Ellwood—whatever she called him—would be arrested and put behind bars where he belonged.

9

———————

Outside the seafood restaurant, where the savory scent of garlic oozed from the building, Travis ended his call with Colonel Vogler. His CO wanted them to wait to report White. To do additional research and see if they could learn more. To see if Nick's report would tie the hack to White.

So Travis had no choice. He would wait. And while he did, he would focus on Robb.

He entered the restaurant albeit reluctantly. After hearing Warren White might be a murderer, Travis hadn't wanted to leave Claire behind. Sure, White was out of town, but guys changed plans all the time. Still, Claire had promised to stay at the institute with Gage, and Travis trusted in Gage's skills to protect her.

He looked around the large dining room. The lunchtime rush was in full swing as tangy spices mixed with the salty ocean smell of seafood scented the air, but Travis had no appetite. Not when he was tracking down the man who could be stalking and could've tried to abduct Claire.

He searched the narrow room overloaded with tree branches and twinkling white lights for the man who resembled Robb's personnel photo. Travis quickly spotted the muscled guy with thinning hair sitting at a long counter near the back. Just seeing the man who was at the very least stalking Claire sent Travis's anger vibrating to a quick boil.

Stop. Breathe. Anger will get you nowhere. You're on a mission. Like any other mission.

He drew in a few cleansing breaths and crossed the room to slide onto a vacant stool next to Robb. He had no telltale marks on his face from Claire headbutting him, but he might not bruise easily. Then again, could Claire really have succeeded in fighting this guy off? He was easily six foot, two hundred pounds of muscle. He clearly still worked out.

Travis tapped a colorful menu lying on the counter. "Can you recommend anything here?"

Robb looked up from his lunch and ran his gaze over Travis.

Here it comes. Travis waited for the guy to blow him off.

Instead, he got a welcoming smile. "For a fellow Army grunt, sure. The crab cakes are great."

"You active duty?" Travis knew the answer, but he wanted to get Robb talking.

"Nah. I decided to take my chances as a civilian." He stabbed his fork into a golden-brown crab cake. "We don't see many uniforms in the Orlando area."

"I'm on assignment but also visiting a woman." Travis leaned closer and gave a conspiratorial wink. "Thought the uniform would impress her, if you know what I mean."

A lecherous grin distorted Robb's face, twisting it into an ugly expression. He was probably thinking about Claire, and Travis wanted to wipe the look off the guy's face.

Robb thrust out his hand. "Mike Robb."

Travis gripped the creep's hand and resisted the urge to twist it around his back and slam him against a wall. Instead, he forced a smile and offered a fake name in the event Robb still talked with anyone at the institute. "Do you live around here?"

"Not far."

"I've heard there's some great nightlife in this part of town," Travis said, hoping to get Robb to divulge his whereabouts the night of the break-in.

"That there is. I can give you the names of the best clubs if you want."

"Sounds like you go out a lot."

"Not usually. My friends don't like clubbing much. But I've been in a funk the last few weeks. Had to go out on my own to drown my sorrows. Been out every night lately."

Which meant he might not have a concrete alibi unless a bartender or waitress could ID him. "Sounds like woman troubles."

"Exactly, but I'm working on a plan to win her over."

Plan? Like stealing her equipment and then pretending to be the hero who finds and returns it? But that wouldn't explain the abduction attempt.

The desire for the answer almost made Travis rush ahead, but he counted a few beats until the urge passed. "I have a good ear if you want to talk about it."

Robb glanced at his watch. "I'd take you up on it, but I have to get back to work."

At the job you no longer have?

Robb pushed to his feet. Travis felt his opportunity slipping away, and yet he didn't want to sound overeager and alert Robb to his real mission. "Maybe some other time then."

Robb tilted his head, and Travis could almost see thoughts pinging through the guy's brain. "I'm going bowling tonight with a couple of friends. If you don't have plans you could stop by."

Perfect. "I'm not sure I'll be free," Travis said, playing it cool. "But give me the details just in case."

Robb rattled off the particulars for a nearby bowling alley as he tossed a meager tip onto the counter. "Maybe I'll see you there."

Robb departed, and Travis's intuition screamed to follow the guy. First, Travis would pocket the plastic glass Robb used to send to Sierra to process the DNA. Travis slipped into the shirt-dampening humidity and waited until Robb climbed into a shiny red sedan before heading to his rental car. He eased into traffic and hung well back from Robb. Fortunately, the red car stuck out in the sea of white rentals populating the tourist capital of Florida, making it a breeze to follow.

Surprisingly, Robb took a direct route to the institute where he pulled to the curb well shy of the guard station. Travis stopped farther back and grabbed binoculars from his bag. He zoomed in on Robb, who'd perched a camera on his open window, aiming it at the institute.

Was he planning an attack here? Or maybe another theft?

Robb continued to snap photos. Time ticking slowly by. Tension mounting. Travis had the urge to march up to Robb and demand an explanation, but he employed the patience he'd learned on the job. That was, until Robb put his camera away. Then Travis gripped his weapon and sat at full alert.

Robb fired up his car and drove slowly past the building. At the corner, he whipped a U-turn and crept by in the other direction. After he cleared the building, and Travis knew Claire wasn't in danger, he dropped down in his seat so Robb wouldn't see him.

Despite the ongoing danger Robb posed to Claire, Travis smiled. Looked like Robb could indeed be their man and not Warren White. Now all Travis had to do was prove it. Starting with sending in the glass for DNA and then a clandestine search of Robb's apartment while he was at the bowling alley.

~

"I'd hoped Nick's report would tell us who stole the software." Claire looked up from pouring over Nick's report to Travis, where he sat across from her at her dining room table.

Travis leaned back in his chair. "And I'd hoped he could at least figure out who reactivated Robb's credentials, but they covered their tracks. At least Nick confirmed the time of the hack and has the hacker's IP address to track down."

"Yeah," Claire said, disappointment settling in. "But he said it was routed through so many different hubs, that he might not be able to get the actual location where the hack originated from."

"Don't give up hope, okay?" Travis smiled. "We know Nick has mad skills, and if it can be traced, he's our guy to do it."

"You're right." She lifted her shoulders. "While you were at lunch with him, I went to see Kent and Alan. I figured if I got a look at them, I might see if I bruised their faces."

"And?"

She shook her head. "Kent was meeting with a supplier offsite, and Alan had no markings."

"Neither did Robb. But that doesn't mean anything. I've seen guys go through more than you put Robb through and come out without a mark.."

"So we keep them all as suspects. I hope your meeting with Mike might bring a lead."

Travis glanced at his watch. "Speaking of which, I need to head out."

She trailed Travis to the front door, her emotions lingering near the surface as they had been since Travis arrived. She still didn't want to be around him, and yet, she didn't want him to leave. What was wrong with her? She needed to get a grip on the situation.

He rested his hand on the knob then faced her, his expression a hazy mix of concern and eagerness to get going. "Be sure to keep the door locked and listen to Gage."

"Relax, I'll be fine," Claire said, though uncertainty continued to crowd her brain. She was thankful for Gage's help. She appreciated his protection, and despite his arm injury, he put in an outstanding performance on the simulations, but she still felt safer with Travis.

She wouldn't keep him here when Mike was waiting at the bowling alley. "You'll be with our top suspect, so he won't be coming after me. I'll be fine."

"Don't let your guard down. I won't have eyes on him until after I get a good look at his apartment while he claims he'll be at the bowling alley."

"I don't think he's lying about that. I know he went bowling every week while he worked with me."

"Still, take care." Travis searched her eyes, and she warmed at his genuine concern. Concern for her. For her safety. She loved that he was always willing to come to the aid of someone in trouble.

Check. Down went another mark in his good-guy column. Even with her desire to keep him at bay, he was quickly swaying her toward thoughts she shouldn't even be considering.

"I hope to be back by ten at the latest." After a final lingering look that did nothing to help Claire forget the effect he had on her, he stepped through the door and closed it firmly behind him.

She twisted the lock as if locking him from her heart then went to the kitchen and retrieved her favorite mug. Gage kept a watchful gaze from a chair by the entrance.

"Cup of hot chocolate or tea? Coffee?" she asked him.

"Nothing for me, but thanks."

She filled her mug with water, and as she dug out a packet of cocoa, Gage bolted from his chair and raced to the front door.

Claire's heart lurched. Had her attacker seen Travis leave and was at the door, planning an attack?

Gage looked through the peephole. "It's Julie."

Claire started for the door.

Gage eyed her. "Step back to the kitchen. I'll let Julie in."

She backed into the small kitchen and waited as Gage opened the door and looked out. "You're alone?"

"Yes," Julie said.

"Then come in." Gage stepped back and secured the door behind Julie.

She came in to the kitchen and frowned.

"Something wrong?" Claire held her mug, ignoring the water waiting to be heated.

"Not with me." Julie dropped onto a counter stool. "But you look worried and makes me think I was even more right about stopping by to see if you were okay since you were attacked."

Claire put the mug in the microwave and stared at the whirling turntable as she considered her answer. Clearly, Claire hadn't hidden her distress over Travis leaving, but Claire still couldn't discuss the theft with her. Did she want to talk about Travis with Julie? Claire had never told anyone, not even her mother, the real reason she'd ended things with him. She'd barely been able to admit it to herself, much less talk about it, but now that he was back and raising all these feelings again, the need to talk about it with someone was pressing in.

Was Julie the right person, though? The line Claire had held with Julie made her unbiased when it came to Travis, and she should be able to offer a rational opinion. Maybe she could help.

"I guess I'm more uncertain than worried," Claire answered, hoping to slide into the discussion and see where it took them.

"Uncertain about your safety or about Travis?"

"Gage's here. He'll keep me safe." Claire waited for the microwave to ding, then took the cup to the breakfast bar.

Julie perched on the edge of her stool and rested her elbows on the smooth granite counter. "I don't know how you can drink that when it's so warm out."

"Comforting, I guess. Growing up in Pittsburgh it was my go-to drink." Claire poured the chocolate powder into the mug.

Julie shifted closer. "This is about Travis, isn't it?"

Claire shrugged, but her reluctance was halfhearted as she really did want to get this out in the open to try to make sense of her feelings. She just didn't know how to begin revealing something she'd kept to herself for so long.

"It's clear you two still have a thing for each other," Julie continued. "So why'd you break up?"

Julie was right. They did still have a thing for each other. Claire had no idea what this thing was, but it was a good place to start the discussion. She perched on a stool and thought back to the beginning—when her father died. Memories flooded back, and she stirred the cocoa to keep from crying. The day of his funeral was as fresh today as it'd been that bitterly cold day years ago. Standing at the freezing cemetery, Claire's arm around her mother's convulsing shoulders as much for warmth as for comfort in their loss. Watching them lower the casket into the ground. Saying good-bye. Forever.

"Claire?" Julie asked gently.

Claire forced herself to move forward. "I told you about how my dad was killed in that chopper crash. Well, I...the pain. It was unbearable."

Julie patted her hand. "I've never lost anyone so unexpectedly, but I can imagine how hard it must've been."

No, you can't. Not really. Not until you experience it. "I vowed to do everything I could to never go through it again. Which meant I couldn't get close to anyone else who served in the military and had a dangerous job like my dad. Then along came Travis." She ended with a lift of her shoulder.

"And you fell for him."

"Big-time." Claire shook her head. "I mean, really! How could I have fallen for a guy who was the worst risk of all? He runs into danger on a daily basis. It's only a matter of time before...well...you know."

"So you broke up with him before that could happen." Julie paused to appraise Claire. "Didn't that hurt too?"

"Yes." Tears pricked Claire's eyes, and she swiped them away. "But not as badly as if I had to say goodbye to him at a funeral."

Julie patted Claire's hand. "Now he's back, and you're still not over him."

"Yes," Claire said as tears began to fall in earnest, and she grabbed a paper towel to dab at them. "But nothing's changed. He's still putting his life on the line, and I'm no more ready to risk the pain of losing him than I was two years ago."

Julie sat back, her eyes narrowing the way they often did when puzzling out a problem at work. "You have to admit if you were going to fall for anyone with a dangerous job,

Travis's skills give him a far better chance of coming home at the end of the day."

Claire hadn't even considered that. "I guess, but skills or not, he's not protected from a rocket launcher or bomb strike."

"I'm so sorry you're going through this. Especially on top of this crazy guy who tried to abduct you." Julie squeezed Claire's hand and seemed sincere, but a mountain of skepticism lingered on her face.

"I hear a 'but' coming."

"Since I'm not a Christian," Julie said, sounding uncertain. "I could be way off base here, but I know you usually pray over big decisions. Have you asked God if He wants you to be with Travis, or did you let your fears get to you and make the decision on your own?"

Claire sat back. A flush of embarrassment heated her face. She'd completely left God out of her problem. Not just once when she ended things with Travis, but for two solid years whenever she'd thought of Travis or about dating. Worse, it'd taken someone who didn't even believe in God to point it out.

How had she been so blind?

She hadn't prayed about the missing prototype either. She'd been so worried about her lost work, and the idea of her project ending up in enemy hands, but she'd never thought to turn it over to God, to trust in His solutions. Or to even consider the idea that He might have sent Travis to her —to protect her work, and to force her to face her fears.

Julie's brows furrowed. "Did I say something wrong?"

"No." Claire shook her head, not only to reassure Julie, but because she couldn't believe how oblivious she'd been. "You said what I needed to hear most, and I'll have to give it some serious thought."

10

Travis slipped through the patio door into Robb's first-floor apartment. Old aluminum sliding door locks like the one installed here were so much easier to bypass than anything else. And he also had the sidewalls of the small patio for privacy. Place was made for burglars.

The cool air conditioning blasted him in the face as he let his eyes adjust to the dimness in the empty dining area. The space was connected to a living room too small for a full-sized sofa. Robb had an old floral loveseat and a TV tray as an end table holding a single bulb lamp with no shade. He clearly was living a sparse lifestyle.

Travis poked his head into the tiny kitchen that smelled like the nutty scent of coffee then went to the first door. Opened it. Closet. Empty. Next door. Bedroom. Heavy drapes pulled.

Travis flipped on the overhead light. He jerked back. Robb had covered the main wall with photos. Newspaper articles. Notes. All about Claire.

Travis fought the urge to turn away. He went closer. Slowly. Step by step. His anxiety rising.

The photos covered every moment of Claire's daily activities. From first dawn to the darkness of night. Shopping. Getting gas. Leaving her home. Arriving at work. Departing. Jogging. Shadows of her body behind closed blinds at her home. And even shots of her at work in her office. That must've happened before he was fired. No. He might have hidden cameras in the office.

Cameras? Fixed on Claire. When she didn't know it. When she innocently went about her day. Being watched by this sicko.

Acid churned in Travis's gut. Burning in his throat. His fist rose instinctively to jab the wall. He held back. Couldn't let Robb suspect anyone had been here. Travis took pictures of the giant collage instead. Far away. Up close. Every angle.

He stowed his phone and studied the notes Robb had posted. They reflected dates and times. And suggested what they would do together when she finally realized she loved him too.

Personal, intimate things Travis didn't even want to contemplate. So he didn't. Hoping to find the prototype, he backed away and searched under the twin bed with a worn striped comforter. Nothing. He searched the closet and then the bathroom vanity, noting a ninety-day prescription for Valium. Why exactly did the guy need Valium on a regular basis? Something else Travis didn't want to ponder.

He returned to the kitchen and checked the cupboards. Nothing but paper dishes, cans of tuna, and microwave macaroni and cheese. The refrigerator was nearly empty save condiments and a large loaf of white bread.

No computer or tablet. Odd for an IT professional. He could keep it locked in his trunk. If he needed to flee he would want the electronic records of the photos he'd plastered all over the wall.

The wall. The sick stalker's wall.

Travis clenched his teeth and turned for the door. GPS had told him that the bowling alley was sixteen minutes away. Sixteen minutes to get his head around the depth of Robb's obsession or else when Travis saw the guy he might just pummel him.

∼

Two hours of bowling and Travis had learned nothing other than Robb was highly competitive and a sore loser. Robb and his friends Hank and Nate had been too busy focusing on one-upping each other to give Travis time alone with Robb to grill the guy.

Travis poured his frustration into the bowling ball and hurled it down the lane. The pins exploded, the loud whack fighting with an instrumental version of "Come Together" blaring from speakers.

Cautioning himself not to gloat over the win and alienate Robb, Travis turned back to the group.

Hank looked at Travis, a snide grin on his chubby face. "So glad you came along so Mike didn't skunk all of us." He slid his ball into a neon-orange tote bag. "I'm out of here. Catch you guys tomorrow."

"Hold up, I'll walk out with you." Nate shrugged into a lightweight jacket, his slight frame the opposite of Hank's.

"Fine, run home to your wives," Robb said tauntingly.

Hank picked up his bag and scowled. "You're just jealous there isn't a little woman waiting at home for you."

Robb fired a testy look at his buddy. "I'll be married soon enough."

"Don't you actually need a girlfriend for that to happen?" Nate asked.

"I've got a girlfriend," Robb ground out between clenched teeth.

"Oh, right." Hank raised his eyes in disbelief. "Claire. The woman we've never even seen."

They know about Claire?

Robb crossed his arms, his jaw rigid. "That doesn't mean she doesn't exist."

"Oh, we think she exists." Nate cast a knowing look at Hank. "We just don't believe she's your girlfriend."

Robb spun on Nate, anger firing from his eyes. Sharp, heated daggers of anger. He was fully capable of hurting someone—maybe even Claire, the woman he claimed to love.

"You'll see." Robb clenched his teeth. "She's not only my girlfriend, but she'll be my fiancée before the week is out."

A timeline? Not one Robb would achieve when Travis was at Claire's side.

"Whatever." Nate rolled his eyes and clapped a hand on Hank's shoulder. "Ready, man?"

Hank nodded, and they strode away.

"Sorry about that." Robb fired off an apology to Travis but kept his flaming, angry gaze on his friends.

Travis slipped out of his bowling shoes. "I have to admit it was uncomfortable."

"They just don't get it. But they will. Everyone will." Robb packed up his equipment. "Once I make Claire mine. For life."

You won't get close enough to make her yours for even a minute.

Robb leaned closer, and Travis had to fist his hands not to deck the guy. "But see, what they don't know is, I've got this big thing in the works that's gonna ensure Claire will marry me."

The soda Travis drank earlier churned in his stomach,

but he swallowed before talking and letting out his disgust for this man. "Big thing? Like what?"

"I don't want to talk about the details. You know, in case I jinx it." Robb winked. "But trust me. It's gonna happen soon. Real soon and she won't know what hit her."

Robb stowed his shoes in his bowling bag and picked it up. "Let's get your shoes turned in and get out of here."

Travis headed to the rental return, questioning Robb on the way, but he'd clammed up. Outside, Travis turned to Robb. "I'll be in town for a week or so. Maybe we could grab a beer."

"Maybe." Robb slid into his car.

Frustrated, Travis stepped back as Robb pulled out. Travis hurried to his SUV and followed Robb's car. It was soon clear he was heading home, but Travis kept on his tail through light traffic on this clear evening. Robb parked in his lot and entered his apartment. Travis hung out for an hour to make sure Robb didn't leave again. Watching and stewing.

He'd been inches from the creep stalking Claire, and Travis had let him walk away. Just like that. No punishment. One of the hardest things Travis had done.

Second only to leaving now without doing anything. He cranked his engine and pointed his SUV toward Claire's place.

Robb's words reverberated through his brain.

Soon. Real soon.

Had Robb really stolen the prototype to stage a phony recovery of the device to garner Claire's favor? Or were his plans more sinister and totally unrelated to the theft?

She's mine. The words shot into Travis's brain. *Whoa, what? Where had that come from?*

Time to admit it. He wasn't over Claire. Far from it. His feelings for her were just as strong as the day she'd rejected him. Could they work things out now? Was he even willing to try after the way she'd let him down? How could he even consider trusting her again when her rejection still stung?

Hah, get a grip. A second chance wasn't for him. Wasn't for most of the guys in his company. Most women couldn't handle a spec ops guy continually leaving at a moment's notice with no idea when they'd return. He didn't like the situation, but he understood. Besides, Claire might be attracted to him, but she'd made it perfectly clear that she wasn't interested in pursuing anything, whether he wanted to or not.

Feeling defeated, he parked in her driveway and knocked on the door.

Gage answered.

"We good?" Travis asked.

"All clear," Gage said.

Travis lowered his voice and shared his findings along with photos from Robb's place.

Gage let out a low whistle. "He's really looking like our guy."

"Yeah," Travis said. "Question is, do I show this to Claire?"

Gage cocked his head. "Keep it from her, and she'll never trust you again."

Travis could barely stomach the thought of hurting her.

"You know I'm right," Gage said.

"I do."

"Then do the right thing, man." Gage clapped Travis on the back. "No matter how much it hurts you."

Travis nodded but not because he liked the decision.

"We'll have to make a plan in the morning on how to handle the guy," Gage said. "For now, I'm gonna head to the bedroom and get a little shuteye before my watch."

"I won't be sleeping," Travis said, knowing full well his

buddy was clearing the stage for Travis to be alone with Claire. Not something that was good for either of them. "So go ahead and turn in for the night."

"I'll see you at zero three hundred as planned, and you can do whatever you want." Gage passed Claire where she sat on the sofa.

She'd curled her feet under her, and her Bible lay open on her lap. She looked at Travis, her expression flat and unreadable. "I was beginning to wonder if you were coming back."

"I could never stay away from you, Claire," he teased to hide the emotional turmoil he knew was coming.

She frowned. "Everything go okay with Mike and his apartment?"

Travis took a breath and sat next to her. He provided the highlights of the photo wall but didn't go into details. He opened his mouth to tell her that he'd taken pictures of the offensive display, but his throat closed around the words, so he clamped it closed.

"You think they're current?" she asked, thankfully not picking up on his angst.

He swallowed a few times. "Could be."

"If only I could see them, I might be able to tell."

Travis had to show them to her. He got that. She could indeed see something that might help them. But he sure didn't want to.

"Travis?" She locked gazes. "Is there something you're not telling me?"

Yeah, I still care for you and don't want to hurt you more.

"You're scaring me." She eyed him. "What is it?"

"I took pictures of the wall."

"So I can see the photos he took." She closed her Bible and clasped her knees. "Show them to me."

"That's not really necessary," he said, trying one last time to spare her the pain. "You get the gist."

She locked gazes with him. "Show them to me, Travis."

He could try again to withhold them, but she wasn't going to give up. That he knew from his time with her in the past. He'd been blind-dropped into war zones. Invaded warring soldiers' territories. Been shot at. Survived IED's. But showing her the photos left him unsettled. It was one thing to take fire himself, but to let her come under fire like this? Sure it wasn't gunfire, but it would hurt all the same.

She rested a hand on his arm. "It's okay. I can handle seeing them."

He hated to break contact with her, but he got out his phone, opened the photo app, and gave it to her.

She studied the screen. Swiped through photos. One at a time. Enlarging and studying them.

She gasped. "Some of these pictures at work are recent." She looked up, her eyes terrified. "How did he...oh, oh! No. No. Hidden camera, right?"

"Looks like it." Travis curled his fingers to his palms, wishing Robb was right in front of them and Travis could feel the sting of his knuckles against the guy's face. "We'll check first thing in the morning. If he placed them there, we can have him arrested."

"But how do we prove he put them there?"

"He's in possession of the photos, which should give the police enough cause to request his phone and computer where the cameras are likely connected."

"But you were in his apartment illegally. We should have no knowledge of the photos and can't even tell the police about them."

"Leave that to me. I'll figure it out," he said with all the confidence he could muster. He wasn't used to having to do everything by the book, but he would somehow get Robb to let him in.

"One thing's clear." She clutched her hands. "I was wrong. He's clearly deranged and has likely been stalking me. But did he steal the prototype?"

"My gut says yes, but I have nothing concrete to base it on. He just seems slimy to me."

"After seeing those pictures, I guarantee he *is* slimy. That doesn't mean he's a thief or even that he attacked me."

"He's our best lead."

"Yes, but we still have Kent and Alan." A smug smile played on her lips. "While you were off playing private investigator, I thought of a way to get their alibis without raising their suspicions."

"How?"

"I'm giving special presents to the team leaders at the party on Saturday to say thank you for successfully concluding this phase of CATS. We can meet with their wives to get gift suggestions and ask a few other questions while we're at it." Her eyes sparkled with enthusiasm for her idea.

Loving her lighter mood, Travis leaned back and relaxed. A notch. Only a notch. He wouldn't let his guard down until Robb was behind bars. "I thought this whole thing with Robb would bother you more."

"I'm trying to do a better job of trusting God." She tapped her Bible, then set it on a nearby cushion. "Can I ask you a question?"

"Sure," he said, not liking the uneasy look on her face again.

She clutched her arms around her stomach. "I've been thinking about when Jeter died."

Jeter. What in the world? Travis focused on her family photos on the sofa table and tried not to remember that day in her office when he'd learned his buddy had died in an ambush. Not remember the pain. The sharp, gut-wrenching pain.

"You were so broken up," she continued. "But then you went on like nothing had happened. You even signed on for another two years."

Because you rejected my proposal that afternoon.

"How can you do that?" Her tone was more accusatory than questioning. "I mean, if I were you, I'd be terrified the same thing would happen to me, and I'd be a basket case on the job."

Where was she going with this? "I won't pretend it's a walk in the park, but there are other teammates counting on us, so we have to move on."

"Then there's your family," she said as if she was speaking her thoughts aloud instead of really talking to him. "I can't imagine what it's like for your mom and dad or even your sister. They must worry all the time, living every day knowing the danger you're in. Wondering if today is the day that..." She jumped to her feet and started pacing.

"Hey." He went to her and turned her to face him. "What's this all about?"

She looked at her feet.

He tipped her face up and found concern and—dare he hope?—caring in her eyes. "Are you worried about me?"

"Maybe. If we ever got..." She paused and inhaled deeply. "I don't know how..."

Had she connected Jeter's death that day with a potential future with Travis, wondering how she might handle it if he were killed in action too?

He had to clarify even if she shut him down again. "Are you saying, if we were together you wouldn't know how to handle being with someone who faces danger every day?"

She nodded. "My mom handled it just fine, but then

Dad hadn't deployed to war-torn countries. But you..." She shrugged and looked like she wanted to bolt.

He took her hand, reveling in the fact that she didn't try to remove it. "I know it's hard on my family. It's hard on all military families when a loved one deploys to a dangerous area. But special forces isn't just a job to me. It's like a calling. I can't see the wrongs of the world and not try to right them. My parents made me who I am today, so they understand that."

"Isn't there another way?" she whispered. "A safer way to do the same thing?"

"Maybe, but right now it's a good fit for me." *At least it was until I discovered how much it bothers you.* "Plus, it helps that we're a family of believers. We try to remember God has a plan and trust Him. Then we let it go."

She stared at him. "You make it sound so easy."

"Easy? No. There are days when bad things happen, and I question everything. But if I let my feelings change my path, then I'm not walking in what I believe is God's will for me."

"I thought I did the same thing. Until tonight." She bit her lip.

"What happened?"

"Julie, of all people, pointed out that I've pretty much failed to trust God since losing my dad." She jerked her hand free and clamped it on the back of her neck. "After he died, the pain nearly broke me, and I wasn't going to go through that again. So without even thinking about what God might want for me, I swore off dating."

His mouth fell open. "What about us? We got together after that."

"We were a mistake." She blinked rapidly. "I didn't mean for it to happen. Quite the opposite."

A mistake. He was a mistake? Fresh pain ripped through him, and he took a step back.

"I'm sorry," she said. "That's how I felt at the time."

"And now?" He forced the question from a dry throat.

"Now? I don't know. I just don't know." She retrieved her Bible, hugged it to her chest like a shield, and without a backward glance, she walked out of the room in much the same way she'd once walked out of his life.

11

The hours inched closer to sunrise, and Travis shifted on the sofa. Gage would be up in an hour for watch duty, and Travis should be tired. But nothing would change the fact that he was in the same house as Claire, leaving him more anxious and distracted than he'd been in a long time. And then there was Robb and what Travis was going to do with the guy. All that weighed on him, and he couldn't sleep even if he wanted to.

Still, he had to get rid of these jitters. Pacing always helped in the past. He swung his feet to the floor and saw the electronic clock on the mantle go out. He looked into the kitchen. Stove. Microwave. All the clocks were black. The house silent.

Like a tomb.

He glanced at the window over the front door. Streetlights were on.

Someone had cut the power

Claire's abductor.

A muffled thump—maybe a window closing or footfalls —sounded from Claire's room.

Travis raced to her door. He heard whisper-soft footsteps

on the other side of her door. Could be Claire checking on the power outage, but he wouldn't risk taking the time to even wake Gage. Mere seconds could prevent a loss of life.

Weapon drawn, he whipped open her door. Moonlight from a skylight bathed over the room, revealing Claire in bed, a man standing near her. One gloved hand held a cloth and hovered near her mouth. A pistol in his other hand was aimed at her head. He shot a look back at Travis.

"What the...?" The intruder dropped the rag and glared at Travis, keeping him locked in place. "Drop your gun or I'll kill her."

Was the voice Robb's? Hard to tell. He was disguising it with a fake high tone. Travis scanned the dark. Tried to make out her assailant's features, but a dark hoodie shadowed his face.

Claire bolted upright in bed, her eyes wide with fear. "What's going on?"

"Relax," Travis said. "I'm here and won't let anything bad happen to you."

She scrambled back against her headboard and clutched her arms around her knees.

His feet fairly throbbed with the need to take action and protect her. But he couldn't hold onto his weapon. No way he would risk her life like that. He slowly laid it on the floor.

"Kick it over here," the guy demanded.

Travis complied. "You don't want to shoot anyone."

He must have agreed as he backed toward the wide-open window.

He'd hefted one leg over the sill. Looked away. A brief moment but long enough.

Travis lunged, grabbing the creep's shoulders and jerking him back inside. He wrestled the man to the ground and caught a glimpse of Claire easing out of bed. "Safe room now, Claire!"

With a roar, the man shot up. Headbutted Travis. Slammed his back into the door. Air gushed from his lungs.

"Gage!" he shouted and held on with one hand, trying to knock the gun free with the other.

The guy twisted his arm out of reach and then heaved his entire weight into Travis's chest, unsettling his feet. He flailed out, but lost his balance and plummeted toward the floor. The intruder lifted his gun, and fearing a shot to the chest, Travis scrambled out of the way. Footfalls pounded behind him, but he got up anyway.

The intruder shoved again. Travis fell. Hit his head on the corner of her dresser, the sound deafening to his ears.

Pain sliced through his skull as darkness beckoned. Sweet, soft, peaceful darkness.

Resist. Claire needs you.

He blinked hard and willed it away. He attempted to get to his feet. Dizzy. The room spinning. The guy shoved past him and bolted through the door.

Travis tried to rise again, but when he heard the front door open, he assumed the attacker had fled. Travis returned his attention to Claire. She crossed the room, a large metal candlestick gripped in her hands, a fierce scowl on her face.

If the situation wasn't so dire, he'd laugh at the comical sight she made holding the candlestick aloft as if it would protect her.

"You won't need that, honey," he forced the words out, the blackness now calling stronger. "He's gone. You should call 911, though." He tried to add a reassuring smile, but the pull of darkness grew, and he let it claim him.

〜

Claire dropped to the floor and found Travis's pulse. Good. He was alive. "Travis. Please. Are you all right?"

Silence.

She checked out his vitals. His breathing was fine. Medics. He needed a medic. She controlled her shaking hands enough to get out her phone and call 911. The operator promised to dispatch an ambulance and officer, and Claire let her phone fall to the floor to turn her attention back to Travis. She slipped her fingers behind his head to lift it to her lap.

Sticky blood coated her fingers. She jerked her hand away, her heart raising in her throat. "No. Oh, no. Oh, no. Please, God, help."

Travis blinked rapidly. His eyes remained open. He started to sit up.

"Don't move," she said, her heart soaring. "Your head's bleeding."

"All the more reason to move so I don't mess up your carpet." A silly grin crossed his face.

If he could joke, he couldn't be hurt too badly.

Gage stumbled into the room, running a hand through his messed up hair. "You two okay?"

"I am," Claire said. "But Travis hit his head and blacked out. Ambulance and police are on the way."

Travis eyed his friend. "You didn't go after the guy?"

Gage huffed out a breath. "Guy got the drop on me. Chloroform, I think."

"Yeah, looked like he planned to use it on Claire too." Travis shifted his focus to her. "We should get you to the safe room while Gage waits for assistance to arrive."

"On it." Gage departed, his steps hesitant and his balance still off.

Travis rolled and staggered to his feet. Claire tried to help him. He shrugged her off. Right. He was a tough guy and wasn't about to accept help. Though he was more wobbly than her shaking knees left her, she let him lead her to the laundry room. She understood his need to protect. It was innate and was the reason he was so good at his job. That coupled with his willingness to put others first were his most endearing qualities.

He reminded her of her father, of all the military men and women she worked with. They'd promised to give everything, including their lives, for service to their country, and her respect for them could not be measured.

His efforts on her behalf reminded her of why she'd fallen in love with him in the first place. If she put the positive traits he'd displayed today in one column and the negative in the other, the positive far outweighed his only negative checkmark for his dangerous job.

But it's a huge negative, she reminded herself before she let his good traits sway her toward making a mistake.

He entered the laundry room after her and twisted the lock behind him. His body was so close in the tiny space she could almost feel his urgency to protect her flowing through him.

A wave of gratitude for Travis's selfless dedication swept over her, and she wanted to throw her arms around him and give him a hug in thanks. Not a good idea.

Think of something else.

He started to run a hand over his head and winced when his fingers grazed the back.

"Sit," she commanded in her best supervisory voice. "I want to look at that cut."

He arched a brow, and she could see he was thinking about disagreeing, so she cast him a stern look.

He laughed, a short burst of surprise that bounced around the small room as he settled on a small bench. "I'm always amazed that a little bit of a thing like you can get so bossy."

"Hey, you grow up in a military household and you learn from the best." She tilted his head and shone her phone's light on his head. Her hand shook from the near attack but she ignored it.

Travis needed her, and she needed to help him. The blood had slowed to a trickle, but she still wanted to apply pressure. She would need a clean cloth for that. She opened her dryer.

"Doing laundry at a time like this?" Travis asked, humor in his tone.

She appreciated his attempt to lighten things up and pulled out a washcloth to display for him. "To stop the bleeding." She moved behind him. "It's gonna hurt."

"In that case." He looked up at her with the little boy grin so in contrast with the big, brawny man that it melted her heart. "Will you hold my hand?"

She laughed and the terror of the night disappeared with it, which she felt certain was his intention. She pressed the cloth against his head, making him wince.

"Sorry," she said. "I hate hurting you when you were injured trying to keep me safe."

"No biggie."

She lifted his chin until she got a good look at his face, and their eyes connected. "It's a big deal to me. You're a wonderful, honorable man who deserves the very best in life, and I know I hurt you. For that I'm so sorry."

He shrugged. "Again, no biggie."

Really? No biggie? She dropped her fingers.

Had he actually moved on so easily when she was still stuck wondering what might've happened if she hadn't broken things off? Maybe he hadn't really cared as deeply for her as she'd believed.

Sadness crept in. Deep aching sadness that she needed to explore. But not now.

Now her full focus needed to stay in the present. On Travis and the man who'd held him at gunpoint and nearly abducted her. If she let her thoughts focus on her feelings and become divided, her attacker might not only succeed in his mission, but he could kill Travis in the process.

A knock sounded on the door.

"We're all clear," Gage said from the other side. "Police are on the way."

Travis opened the door. "We'll stay here until they arrive. Just to be safe."

Gage arched an eyebrow. "It's time we bring in reinforcements."

"What do you have in mind?"

"I'll fly a couple of my guys out here as soon as possible."

"Make it happen," Travis said without consulting her. "Make sure Jackson is one of those guys."

"Already planning on bringing in my spec ops guys, which includes former ranger Cooper Ashcroft. Coop's as solid as Jackson."

"Thanks, and let me know when the police arrive."

She appreciated their decisiveness. She didn't need to be consulted on her security plan. Not when she didn't know a thing about protecting herself against such a foe other than to listen to Travis and Gage.

Visions of waking to find the man standing over her played in her head. She forced her thoughts away. She wouldn't argue with additional support. Not after that.

Travis closed the door and turned to her. "Not that I'm going to change my mind, but are you good with the extra guys?"

She nodded. "But what about your CO?"

"We don't have to read the guys in on the theft. At least

not at the beginning. All they need to know is that you're being stalked and need protection twenty-four/seven."

The intensity in his tone took her back, and she didn't know what to say. Nothing in life had prepared her on how to survive an unknown man targeting her. Thank the good Lord that He sent Travis to her.

"Thank you for being here for me, Travis." A shudder came on her, and no matter how hard she tried to stop the shaking and the tears that were pricking her eyes, she couldn't.

"Hey. Hey." Travis circled his arms around her and drew her close. "I'm sorry. I just failed you."

"You couldn't help it."

"I should've let him go when he was climbing out the window. But I wanted him behind bars."

"You did what I would've done."

"But I brought him back into the room. That's on me."

She remembered Travis lying on the floor and shivered again.

"Don't worry, honey," he said. "Everything will be okay. It won't just be me and Gage, but you'll have four spec ops guys on your side. No one is going to get to you."

She leaned back. "And you? Who will protect you?"

He brushed the hair out of her face and cupped her cheek. "No need to worry about me. This is the sort of thing I'm trained to handle as are the other guys. We'll have each other's backs."

Spec ops guys were well-trained. She got that. But that did not make them invincible. Especially if a former spec op guy was her stalker. Her attack proved Travis was just a man and vulnerable.

Only God could make him invincible.

Please. Please. Don't let anyone get hurt or worse yet—die.

12

Claire held her hand over her eyes against the usual Florida sun outside her office the next morning as Gage and Travis escorted her inside. Temperatures were already approaching ninety and the day had just begun. She wished she could take a dip in the community pool like she did most days in the summer, but Travis would forbid such a public appearance. Not that she would even ask him to let her go. She was too afraid to be out in the open.

They went to her office, her staffers watching carefully. Not because of her. That she was certain. But because of the two intense men accompanying her. She went straight to the chair behind her desk, and instead of taking his usual seat on the corner of her desk, Travis started searching her bookshelves. He didn't have to tell her what he was doing. He was looking for hidden cameras. The angle of the pictures suggested the bookshelves were the most likely location.

Gage closed the door behind them and joined Travis.

She couldn't watch as they ferreted out the offending camera, so she opened her email.

She gasped.

Travis looked over his shoulder. "What is it?"

She pointed at the screen.

Travis was leaning over her shoulder in a flash, his fresh scent doing nothing to still her racing heart. He mumbled something under his breath.

Gage turned to face them. "What's going on?"

"A picture of Claire in her bed along with a warning to stop investigating the theft and to provide the sender with the missing code or he'll kill her."

Gage frowned. "We need Eryn or Nick to trace that email. Getting them down here would take time so they'll just have to do it remotely."

"But there's no remote access," Claire said.

"No problem," Gage said. "They both have the skills to hack your network."

Claire blinked at Gage. "But—"

"But nothing. There aren't many impenetrable networks out there." Gage gave her a conciliatory smile. "At least I know Eryn has never come across a network she couldn't hack. I'm guessing the same is true for Nick. And that it would take less time than a flight down here."

Claire sighed. "That's most disheartening."

"Agreed," Gage said. "But the good news is there aren't enough hackers out there to attack all networks. And of course, big business uses white hat hackers to do penetration testing and analyze security gaps within a computing system."

"Sounds like you've dealt with this before," Travis said.

Gage nodded. "A couple of investigations. Eryn's top-notch in this area, but she would understand if you decided to use Nick."

"He's still trying to trace that IP address," Travis said. "Would be good to keep him on that."

"Agreed," Claire said.

"Don't touch anything else on your computer, and I'll get Eryn on board." Gage dug out his phone and made the call.

"I'm going to find that camera." Travis went back to the bookshelves.

She stepped over to him.

He looked over his shoulder. "I can do this alone if you want."

"I can't just sit there and do nothing." She started pawing through the many books and binders filling the tall bookcase.

They worked side-by-side as Gage talked with Eryn.

"Got it." Travis pulled down a stuffed bear.

"No," she said backing up from the bear. "Not in the bear."

Travis looked at her. "Sentimental?"

"A little girl gave it to me when our team supported a walkathon for the Make a Wish Foundation."

"I'm sorry, honey," he said. "It's got to make things worse."

She drew in a breath. "We have to make sure he pays for this."

"We will." Travis turned his attention back to the bear. "Camera's in his nose. Mind if I take the bear apart?"

"Mind? I do, but go ahead. Figure out how he's doing this." She wrapped her arms around her waist and worked hard not to cry. She wasn't usually a crier, but this was all getting to be too much. Each strike and her vulnerability rose.

He took the bear to the desk and pulled a folding knife from his pocket. He sliced along the back.

"Don't worry. No bears will be hurt today." He smiled. "Just cutting stitches that were applied after the camera was placed."

She returned his smile but she had to force it. She didn't

like this privacy invasion one bit but continued to watch as he lifted a camera from the back of the bear.

Gage shoved his phone into his pocket and looked at Claire. "Eryn's onboard. She's sending a phishing link in an email to you. Click on it as soon as you get it, and she can be in the network in seconds. However, she says it's likely your network manager will be notified of this intrusion soon, but she might be able to check out files before he shuts her down. Then she'll have to come here to access the files internally to keep from raising red flags."

Travis looked up. "Pretty soon your whole team will be here."

"Everyone but Riley and Alex," Gage said. "Gotta leave someone there to man the compound."

"I'm not big on military style compounds, but after hearing about your operation, I would like to see it sometime."

"You're welcome any time. We have some nice guest cabins you could stay in." Gage smiled, probably thinking she would never take him up on it.

But she honestly thought it might be nice to get away from here when this was over. To rest. To recuperate from the shock and fear. Why not visit then? Of course, she saw herself there with Travis—not alone.

"Eryn also said she finished her background report on Norton and is sending it to us, but there were zero red flags on him."

"Not even his finances?"

He shook his head. "Guy looks solid on paper."

Claire frowned. "I was hoping for something to go on, but I guess if it existed, Eryn would have found it."

She would," Gage said. "We'll need a cover story for her while she's here."

"What's her background besides IT?" Travis asked, his focus back on the camera.

"Former FBI agent. Worked cybersecurity."

"Why'd she leave?" Travis asked.

"Got her hand slammed in a door on a raid. Took away her ability to clench her fist or grasp objects as well. The FBI wouldn't risk the potential liability from an injury like that, so they benched her."

Claire couldn't imagine losing her profession just because she hurt her hand. "That's rough."

Gage nodded. "She could've taken an analyst job at the FBI, but she wanted at least the hope of some adventure. So she left."

Claire was impressed at her willingness to follow her passion. "And sounds like she found that adventure with your team."

"She did." Gage lifted his shoulders. "I'm glad to give her the chance to chase her dreams again."

Travis didn't speak but cast a proud look at his buddy.

"The FBI angle won't help here," Claire said. "But since she'll be working on the network, why don't we say we hired a white hat hacker to try to penetrate the network. If that's even possible without remote access."

"It's possible," Travis said. "You all get email and access the Internet through your LAN so a hacker could find his way into even a secured LAN just like Eryn's going to do."

"Okay, then she'll be a hacker," Claire said.

"You can do that without your network security manager's buy-in?" Gage asked.

She nodded. "Normally, I wouldn't, but, yeah, I'll go rogue."

"Claire Reed going rogue?" Travis grinned at her. "Never thought I'd see the day."

She rolled her eyes. "I'm not that straightlaced."

"Umm. Yeah, you are. And that's one of the things I like about you. You think in black and white, not grays, just like me."

She blushed at his compliment. "Then we're agreed. Eryn will pose as a white hat hacker."

Gage held up his phone. "I'll text her in case she needs to bring anything with her to support her cover."

"Okay, got it." Travis looked up. "The camera records the footage and stores it locally. However, it's programmed to transmit the data at specific intervals."

"Which means what?" Gage asked.

"That Robb would have to have access to the network and be within range to receive the data at these times. I've turned it off but we'll need to look for others."

"He had to have access to this office to put the camera in the bear," Gage said.

Travis nodded. "Or take the bear out and return it without raising Claire's suspicions."

"I lock the office when I'm gone. Opens only with my key card."

"Then he likely hacked the key card database and changed his permission," Travis said.

"That wasn't covered in Nick's report," Gage said. "We can have Eryn look into it while she's here."

Claire nodded, but this was one of those things where she wanted to know an answer and yet she didn't. At the moment she wasn't quite sure which one would win out.

Gage's phone chimed, and he glanced at it. "My guys get in around eleven. They'll each get a rental vehicle, but I'll want to brief them right away and put them into action."

"If they'll be onsite we can use the same CATS testing cover story for them too," Claire said. "Means they'll have to run at least one scenario."

"No hardship there." Gage grinned, and she could easily

imagine this good-looking man breaking hearts all across the world, though since losing his wife, he might not be open to a romantic involvement.

She sat behind her desk. "After we finish the camera sweep, I'd hoped to visit Kent's and Alan's wives to see if I could confirm alibis this morning. But I know you're going to say that it's not a good idea, and I honestly agree."

Travis's eyes widened. "That's great, because I'd have to say no. It would be a different story if Gage's men were here. But then I don't think you'll want to show up at these houses with the four of us. Would raise a lot of questions."

She hadn't thought of that aspect. "I guess I can call them."

Travis leaned closer. "What about doing a video call? Gives you a better chance to see if they're lying."

"Good idea." And a suggestion she should expect from a guy who was trained to tell if others were lying to him.

"Since you've got this under control." Gage pushed off the door. "How about I check in with Eryn to give her the updated details and then run a simulation?"

"That would be great. I'll text Julie to watch for you." Claire got out her phone and sent the text while Gage and Travis exchanged a cryptic look.

Did she even want to know what that was all about? Likely not. If they thought she needed to know something, surely they would tell her.

Perfect, came Julie's reply.

Claire looked at Travis. "Do you want to sit in on my calls?"

"If it's okay with you. I might pick up on something you miss."

"Then grab a chair while I get Inez Babbit on my iPad. It's connected via our phone company, so it should be secure."

He grabbed the side chair and brought it around the table.

She placed her iPad on the stand but before connecting the call, looked for an email from Eryn and clicked on the link. "It's weird to click on this knowing it will give someone access to the network when we're all so careful here not to do that."

"I suspect there will be a lecture forthcoming from your network manager."

"He'll enjoy every minute of it." She laughed and connected the call.

Claire hadn't even spoken a word to Inez today, and she already felt like a liar. Sure, she really did want gift ideas, but she could probably come up with something and wanted an alibi for Alan even more.

Inez was about five seven or so and a little plump, but the gaunt woman who answered barely resembled the Inez Claire knew. She was wearing a stocking cap and heavy sweater even in the heat of July.

"Claire." She gave a genuine smile. "What's up? It's not Alan, is it? He's okay?"

"He's fine, " Claire said. "I was hoping I could talk to you a minute about my plan for the company anniversary party."

"Sure." She shifted her focus to Travis.

"This is Travis Chapman," Claire said. "He's one of the soldiers who's participating in our program, and he's helping me with planning."

If she found that odd, she didn't let it show.

"My strength isn't what it used to be, so let me just take a seat." Inez spun and took off down a hallway at a surprising clip.

Claire had never been to the traditionally furnished home before and liked catching a glimpse of it on the screen. They had good taste and looked like expensive taste at that. Even without medical bills, decorating this home could've put them in debt.

"Your house is beautiful," Claire said. "How long have you lived there?"

"Not even two years." Inez frowned. "It was supposed to be our forever home, but..." She shrugged, and her eyes got glassy with tears.

"How are you doing?" Claire asked, even though she wanted to avoid this topic.

Inez just shook her head.

"Is there anything I can do?" Claire asked.

"No, but thank you for always letting Alan off work when I need him. He's been my rock. Holding my hand through all the nausea from chemo. I don't think I could've made it through this last week if he hadn't been here with me every night."

Claire cast a quick, knowing look at Travis, and he gave a clipped nod that was barely perceptible. Claire's work was basically done here. They had a solid alibi for the break-in. Not the attack though.

Inez sat in a wooden dining chair and took a long breath. "I imagine you've seen how tired he's been at work this week. I hope you won't hold that against him. He stayed by my side from sundown to sunup every day and got little sleep. And he takes me to every doctor's appointment. But then you probably know that since he has to miss work a lot. Tuesday's appointment was particularly long. I'm sorry about that."

"Don't be sorry." Claire hated even more that she had an ulterior motive here, but had to admit she was glad that Inez laid it all out there so Claire could forget about Alan as a suspect and actually focus on the gift. "He's a good man."

"The best." A sweet smile crossed her face. "Today seems better for me so maybe we can both sleep tonight."

"I'll pray that happens."

Inez sniffled. "Now you said something about the anniversary. I'm hoping I can come to the party."

"I hope you can too." Claire shared her bogus reason for the call. "Since these gifts are a surprise, I'm enlisting the help of spouses. Can you think of anything Alan has been wanting but wouldn't buy for himself?"

Inez settled a blanket around her frail shoulders. "All of our money and time has gone to this stupid cancer, so he really hasn't had any wants outside of my healing and comfort."

As a caregiver, he needed support too, but there were often no funds for such a thing. "What about a massage? Would he like that, do you think?"

"Oh, yes." Inez's eyes lit up. "That sounds perfect. Something he would never do himself but would be great to help him relax. If I can convince him to leave me alone long enough to go."

"What if I made it a couple's massage?"

"That's very generous of you."

"It's the least I can do for his wonderful work." Claire smiled. "I won't take up any more of your time. I hope you'll be able to come to the party."

"I hope so too." Inez's sadness returned.

Claire hated ending the call and vowed to do more for this couple in the future. "Please don't tell Alan about my call today. The gifts are a surprise."

Inez mimicked zipping her lips.

Claire quickly ended the call, feeling like she was running from this sick woman. And maybe she was. Her prognosis wasn't good, and Claire, like most people, didn't like to look death in the face.

She battled back tears and looked at Travis. "I feel bad for bothering Inez when she's so sick."

"Me too." Travis leaned back in his chair and clasped the back of his neck. "Cancer's rough. I'll be praying for them both."

"Now Sylvia Norton's another story. I never thought I'd feel sorry for Kent, but every time I see Sylvia, I do."

Travis tilted his head. "Why's that?"

"She has everything money can buy. Diamonds. Expensive clothes. A decorator condo. And yet she wants more. Let me get her on a call and you'll see."

Claire looked up the number in Kent's personnel record and then tapped the screen.

The blond with even lighter highlights and makeup that was perfectly applied to accentuate her big eyes and full lips accepted the call. "Oh, Claire. My call just said the institute. I thought it was Kent."

"Sorry to disappoint." Claire smiled.

"I didn't say I was disappointed. Not with that eye candy sitting beside you." She flashed a wide smile at Travis.

Travis cringed, but Claire ignored it. "This is Travis Chapman. He's participating in our program, and he's helping me with the anniversary party planning."

"You're not like any party planner I've ever seen." She winked at Travis.

Claire felt his whole body stiffen next to her, which Sylvia seemed to ignore. She lifted her hand and looked at her manicured pink nails. "What can I do for you, Claire?"

Claire explained the bogus reason for the call. "Can you think of something Kent might want but not buy for himself?"

"No. He pretty much just gets whatever he wants. If you'd asked me a few weeks ago I'd suggest dance lessons."

She ran her hands down her body. "I stay in shape by dancing and would love to share it with Kent."

"You don't think that's a good idea now?" Travis asked.

"Not since *she*." Sylvia shot an angry look at Claire. "Changed the schedule and Kent works most nights now."

Claire glanced at Travis. He knew they didn't have any staff on duty at night and when Claire opened her mouth to tell Sylvia that, Travis mimed keeping her mouth shut.

"Doesn't he have any free nights?" Travis asked casually.

"Ask her." Sylvia jerked her head at Claire. "She makes the schedule."

"Sounds like dance lessons aren't a good idea right now then. Do you have another one?"

"I don't know. He *will* have more money now he's been working nights at the institute."

Nights again?

Maybe Claire could use that to get to the alibi she needed for the attack. "I suppose that's why he wasn't at work Tuesday morning."

"He was there." Sylvia snapped forward in her chair. "At least he said he was."

Claire held up a hand. "Relax. Probably my mistake, and I just didn't see him."

"I hate the night work, but I have to admit that overtime pay is going to be nice to have." She relaxed her shoulders, almost bare under the white tank top straps. "He even promised me a new emerald ring I've been eyeing for putting up with him being gone so often."

"But you can't think of anything *he* might want?" Travis asked.

Claire wanted to probe the night thing first before moving on. "I—"

"Let's give Sylvia a chance to share her thoughts," Travis

interrupted and followed it with a visual plea that Claire couldn't ignore.

Sylvia didn't catch their interaction and started throwing out gift ideas.

"Will one of these ideas work for you?" Travis asked Claire.

"Yes," Claire said, but she had no intention of buying any one of them as each one would benefit Sylvia in some way.

"I mean that's all I got anyway," Sylvia said. "Once you've been married for ten years like us, you don't even discuss those things. So no. I got nothing else for you."

But he knows you want a very pricey ring. Of course, Claire didn't say that aloud. She had far more tact than that. "Okay, thanks, and sorry to disturb."

Sylvia leaned forward, accentuating her cleavage and eyeing up Travis. "Bye, sugar. Don't be a stranger."

Claire ended the call.

Travis mimicked a shudder. "I couldn't wait for you to end that call."

"She does have a real ick factor going on, but what do you think about her claim that Kent's been working nights at the institute?"

"We both know there aren't any night shifts. So either she lied to us or Kent lied to her about where he's been at night."

"How do we figure out which one of them is telling the truth?"

"Doesn't matter. What's important is where he's been going at night. I'll follow him tonight to find out."

Claire hated the thought of Travis going out again tonight, but at least he wasn't going to some warring country. "Maybe Kent's leaving home to get away from her."

"Could be." He held her gaze. "It's equally as likely that he's working a second job, trying to make enough money to keep her happy. And that makes him an ideal person to steal and sell an expensive prototype."

Travis's dire tone settled over her as her phone rang, making her jump. She looked at Caller ID. "It's the police department." She put the call on speaker.

"Dr. Reed, this is Detective Purcell." Tension deepened his voice. "We've finished running the tests on the cloth recovered at your house after the break-in. As we suspected, it was saturated with chloroform."

Just like Travis had suggested, and Claire wasn't surprised to hear such news. The scent of the sweet-smelling compound came back. As did the memory of the man's hand hovering over her mouth. Her hand trembled, and she clasped it in her lap to keep Travis from seeing her unease. "So we're looking for someone with access to chloroform then."

"Unfortunately it's often used as a solvent in laboratories and readily available." He paused for a moment. "Perhaps you know someone with access to a lab."

A lab? Her heart sank.

"Can you hold for a second?" She muted her phone and looked at Travis. "Mike Robb minored in chemistry in college. Maybe he has access to a lab through a friend or an old classmate. Should I tell Purcell?"

"No." Travis met her gaze, his intensity scaring her even more. "If you tell him, he'll question Robb, and that might spook the guy. The last thing I want is for that jerk to move up plans that we can assume are meant to cause you harm."

Travis was right. They were barely staying one step ahead of the creep trying to abduct her. If it *had* been him in her bedroom, he'd come close to harming both her and Travis, and she wouldn't do anything to cause him to escalate these attacks.

13

_____

Wishing coffee could bring him to life after his late night, Travis downed the last swallow of his fourth cup of the day and tossed it in the break room trash. He'd hung outside Kent Norton's house until three a.m., but the guy didn't leave home. A major disappointment. It was bad enough that Travis sat in a stifling hot car for endless hours, but seeing Claire's expression fall this morning when he'd told her they were no closer to finding her attacker? That cut right through him.

But it was soon replaced by shock when Colonel Lynch asked to see him in his office. Travis didn't know what to expect with the colonel in charge of the institute, but the impromptu demand by Lynch for Travis to hightail it to his office had him double-timing it down the hallway.

Travis straightened his tie and knocked on the door.

"Enter," the colonel's rumbling voice sounded.

Thinking Lynch would ask for an update on the theft, Travis mentally prepared and pushed through the doorway to stand at attention and salute.

"At ease." Lynch pointed at his side chair. "Sit."

"Yes, sir." Travis took a seat but was far from easy.

Lynch rested his elbows on the desk and steepled his fingers. "How's the investigation going?"

Travis brought him up to speed.

"You know, Chapman, I've been thinking. It would be good to have a soldier of your resources around here on a permanent basis."

Travis worked hard not to gape at the colonel. "Permanent?"

"You blow the testing scenarios out of the water and are the best one to evaluate the software. I know Dr. Reed waits for soldiers to be available for testing and having you on site could speed the software development along."

"Not sure that would be a full-time job."

"No, but there are other issues here at the institute that I could use your help on. I'm not at liberty to share them right now, but I know they'll be challenging to you."

Travis was fully unprepared for this offer and honestly didn't know what to say. "I appreciate the offer, sir, and I will consider it. But I don't know if I can leave the team."

"I can understand that, but you, like every other operator, will age out and need to leave at some point in the not-too-distant future." Lynch stood. "Think it over and get back to me soon."

Travis shot to his feet. "Yes, sir."

He marched out of the office and considered leaning against the wall to think. He never expected the colonel to offer him a job. But he had. A full-time one. Right here at the institute.

With Claire.

Not like it mattered. After her abrupt end to him holding her last night, he doubted she would want him around.

But if God wants you to be together, it can happen. Oh, wow. That came out of nowhere.

During Travis's restless night, he'd pondered Claire's

revelation about ignoring God. Maybe Travis had been doing the same thing. He'd been certain that being a Green Beret was the life God wanted him to lead, but had God really kept him there, or had Travis decided for himself that he should stay? And was it possible that this was the point where God wanted him to take a different fork in the road?

Valid questions needing answers—later—when he had time to sort them out. Much later, when Claire wasn't waiting for him. He started down the deserted hallway to Claire's office so he could drive her home.

She looked up from stowing her laptop. "Right on time."

"On time for what?"

"Doesn't look like we'll have this solved by tomorrow, so I wanted to talk about my visit to the party venue tomorrow."

All thoughts of a possible future together fled at the mention of her stepping into a potentially dangerous situation. "I know you really want to hold this party, but it's not a good idea. You'll be too exposed. Anyone could attempt an abduction."

She wrinkled her nose at him. "Only a few people know we'll be going there tomorrow, and between you and Gage's men, you can be sure no one follows us."

She had a point, but... "Can't this wait until the thief is apprehended?"

"Who knows how long that'll take? We're no closer to resolving this case than when we started, and I won't let it ruin things to honor the members of our team." She took a stubborn stance.

She looked like a young girl standing up to her parents. He gritted his teeth before her adorable expression had him yielding without thinking this through.

She took a few steps closer to him. "Next you'll tell me I can't go to church on Sunday if this isn't over by then."

"Now you're just trying to make me feel guilty."

An impish smile crossed her face. "Is it working?"

"Yes," he reluctantly admitted.

"So we can go to the venue?" She came even closer, the plea in her eyes making him want to give in.

Despite the heady effect she continued to have on him, he wasn't ready to concede. Not without doing a bit of recon first. "Give me the address. I'll check satellite photos and then Gage and I'll do some recon on the place before I take you home. If I think it's safe, then we'll go."

A jubilant smile brightened her face, and she threw her arms around his neck, hugging him hard. She felt warm and soft and smelled of springtime. He should push her away until he could be sure God really was telling him to pursue her again, but he couldn't think straight with her in his arms.

He wanted to have her in his life again. Wanted sunshiny mornings with her smiling at him in a cozy home. Their home, with cookies baking in the oven and children with Claire's bright smile sitting down to sample them. How cheesy was all of that? Not something he would ever admit aloud. Not even to her. And if anyone accused him of thinking this way, he would deny it. But...that's what he wanted. It was clear to him now.

For the first time since she'd sent him packing, he had hope. Nothing was clear yet, but he was willing to consider a leap of faith. Consider that God might work this out for the two of them. Claire was more than worth it.

Travis and Gage walked the venue with an event coordinator named Michelle. Travis didn't really want the venue to be safe for a visit. He wanted to keep Claire at home or at the institute where she would be safe, but with Gage and his men in town, they could secure the place if Claire used the entrance closest to the party room.

Travis stepped away from the perky events manager, who'd been flirting from the moment they'd arrived. She seemed to like the uniform more, so had set her focus on Travis. Which he found tiring.

He joined Gage by the room entrance.

"Looks good, right?" Gage asked.

"Right. With your guys here, we can defend the place." *Defend Claire.*

"But even with the best defense, things could go wrong." Gage stared at him. "You willing to risk that?"

"I don't think we have a choice." Travis planted his hands on his hips. "I can't lie to Claire. If I say it's defensible and don't let her go, then she finds out I lied, I doubt she'd ever talk to me again."

"And it's clear you want to do some talking in the future." Gage laughed.

Travis rolled his eyes. "Your men can check everyone at the door. Tactfully, of course."

"Of course. We're not all barbarians in the Pacific Northwest." Gage grinned.

"So the rumors aren't true, then?" Travis laughed.

"Not all of them." Gage's smile widened.

Travis appreciated his buddy lightening up the mood as Travis was intense far too much of the time. "You can post them at the service door. Keep an eye on catering staff."

"And it's a given that you'll be glued to Claire's side."

"Yeah, if she allows it."

"You'll just have to let go of your attraction for the woman for a moment to convince her of the necessity of close protection." Gage eyed him. "You mix that in with your request, and she won't buy it."

Gage was right. But that didn't mean Travis could pull it off.

You have to, man. Her life could depend on it.

A thought that kept pounding in his head all the way back to the institute, where they found her in the observation room watching Jackson run a jungle scenario.

They didn't talk but just stood behind her to observe Jackson battle his way through the jungle while Coop sat on a stool looking bored. They both wore khaki cargo pants. Coop had chosen an Army green performance T-shirt that a lot of guys on the teams wore, and Jackson had on a black one.

"He's looking good," Gage said. "If you ignore the way he babies that right knee."

Travis nodded. "It's gonna cost him on time."

"He's still running faster than a lot of the others who've run this scenario." Claire looked over her shoulder. "Most of them let the jungle overgrowth slow them down, but not the spec ops guys. You barrel right through it."

"Comes with being trained on spatial awareness," Travis said. "You learn to quickly assess what's a danger to you and what's not."

She turned fully. "Like visiting the venue?"

"Not really," he said. "That was recon. A different animal."

She kept her focus pinned to Travis. "And what did this animal tell you?"

"That we'll be visiting the venue tomorrow and for the party. If you still need us then, we'll be there for you." He wanted to add that he wanted to be there for her beyond then, but he wouldn't get into a private discussion with Gage in the room.

She peered at Gage. "You agree?"

"I do. We can button that place up pretty easily as long

as you let my guys check ID's against a guest list at the door."

She tilted her head. "It'll be odd, but I can agree to that."

She faced Travis again. "Any other requirements?"

"Gage will be at the service entrance that night to keep watch, and I'll be with you. And I mean with you. You go nowhere except into the restroom without me, and even then, we check it out in advance."

She narrowed her eyes. "In that case, I suggest you attend as my date so we can explain why you're sticking so close to me."

"Um...yeah...yeah, that would work." He could barely get his head around her agreeing to this and even embracing it.

"You'll all need civilian clothes for this event, and it's formal."

"I should be able to manage that," Travis said. "As long as I can find a formal wear rental place that caters to guys our size."

"Coop hates formal wear, so I'll put him on finding a place." Gage laughed.

Claire shook her head. "You're so mean."

"He'll get me back." Gage sounded confident in his take and not at all upset. "This is just the kinds of thing guys in the teams do."

Travis's phone rang. "It's Sierra."

He answered and put her on speaker.

"The DNA has come back for the samples we recovered at the institute," she said. "That includes the Band-Aid wrappers and bloody tissue. Unfortunately, it didn't return a match to anyone in the federal database and it's too soon to compare to the one you overnighted from Mike Robb. Our DNA team will compare it as soon as it finishes processing, which will be sometime tomorrow."

"Anything else produce a lead?" Travis asked, hoping for a yes.

"Not yet. We had zero matches on the fingerprints in databases. Something we all expected, but we're still comparing fingerprints to the staff. The most promising would have been from the keyboard in the server room, but Warren White's prints were the only ones lifted, and he has reason to be using that computer."

"He does, but he's also on our radar as a potential suspect," Travis said. "We'd get you his DNA but he's out of town, and honestly, finding his DNA on the keyboard doesn't help since he has authorization to be in the server room."

"Right," she said.

"Anything else to share?" Travis asked.

"As you can imagine, we lifted a large number of prints in the public areas, which we haven't yet finished. It's a time-consuming task as it's a manual process."

"Thank you for keeping after it," Travis said.

"We hope to finish today, and I'll let you know what we find." Sierra ended the call.

"We keep striking out," Claire said.

"I prefer to look at it as we're just eliminating leads so we can focus on the right ones," Travis said.

"And that's what makes you a good operator," Gage said. "You keep looking forward."

Travis wasn't so sure about that. For work, yeah. In his life with Claire, no. He needed to change that. God would want him to look forward unless he was looking at the past to reminisce over good things. Or to see how God had been faithful. How He'd brought Travis through so many trials. He would bring him through this one and show him the way with Claire, wouldn't He?

The computer sounded an alarm, and Claire turned

back to it. "Jackson's done. Coop chose to run the desert scenario. I didn't pick up on any obvious injury for him and he ran it in record time."

"It's his back," Gage said.

"You mean he did better than me?" Travis asked.

"He did better than both of you."

"Oh, man." Gage ran a hand over his head. "I'll never live that down. Letting an Army grunt beat me."

"Well, I've always told you Army is superior, but..." Travis laughed.

Claire rolled her eyes and pressed the speaker button for the simulation room. "Go ahead and come on in here. Please bring the virtual device with you."

Jackson and Coop entered the observation room.

"Tell me I bested this guy's score," Jackson said to Claire the moment his foot crossed the threshold and clapped Travis on the back.

"Sorry."

Jackson's shoulders dropped. "I guess I shouldn't have expected it with this bum leg, but..."

"Hey, man." Travis chest bumped Jackson. "You wouldn't have beaten me even if you were fully able."

Jackson socked Travis in the arm.

Claire looked at Coop. "Did you want to know about your score?"

Coop shrugged half-heartedly. "Sure, yeah, if you want to tell me."

"Better than Gage and Travis both," Claire said.

Did Travis note a hint of enjoyment in her tone?

"Nice," Coop said and then looked at Gage. "But I mean, how much of an achievement is skunking an OG like you."

"Old guy? I don't think four years difference in our ages qualifies me as an OG, but whatever." Gage laughed.

"It's nearly impossible to best me at anything, so

congrats." Travis held out his hand to Coop. "Travis Chapman."

"Cooper Ashcroft. Former Ranger." He punished Travis's hand with his grip. "Gage sang your praises. Maybe too much. So what are you not telling us?"

"I'm just that fine." Travis laughed.

"I don't think I can survive all this testosterone in the room." Claire waved a hand in front of her face and laughed. "I hate to break up the party, but I need things secured for the night, and I really want to get out of here."

Travis was unreasonably proud of her for holding her own with the guys. But then she dealt with tough guys all the time in testing, so this was nothing different.

She took the virtual device from Jackson.

"We'll bring a car around," Gage said. "And let's keep your stalker guessing by using the back entrance tonight."

She held up the device. "I just have to lock this up and grab my things, and then I'm ready."

The guys departed.

Travis stayed behind. "I'll accompany you."

"I'm pretty sure I'm safe in the building."

"I know. Just humor me." He looked her in the eye. "It'll be good practice for Saturday night."

She started down the hallway, and he followed. "I don't need practice to be close to you. I once wanted nothing more than that."

"Me too."

He tugged her to a stop. "Why did you really end things, Claire? Was it the job? Your fear of losing me? You didn't love me? What?"

"All of it except loving you, but I honestly couldn't see how we could be together when we lived in different states and neither of us wanted to give up our jobs."

"Wanted to or is it still want?"

"I can't leave this program. Maybe two years from now when we're scheduled to complete, but not now." She started walking again. "So nothing has changed, has it?"

"No, nothing." He tried to hide his sadness, but Claire's assessing gaze said he probably didn't manage it.

Julie stepped out of a room and nearly plowed into Claire. "Oh, hey. Glad I bumped into you. I was thinking after Coop's trial that our guinea pigs aren't in uniform, and you didn't mention their branch."

"They're both former spec ops guys."

Julie eyed Claire. "Why all the former guys instead of active duty all of a sudden?"

"Are you kidding me?" Claire tried to sound natural, but it was hard when this was another half-truth. "You know the active guys deploy at a moment's notice, and our tests come second. How many times have we been waitlisted from that, and then they never show?"

"Gotcha. Former means available."

Travis was glad Julie caught on, and Claire didn't have to outright lie.

Claire nodded. "I didn't get a chance to have them fill out the registration packets with confidentiality agreements. Could you print them out for me, and I can get them signed?"

"Yes, but then I'd like to go. Eric and I have plans to see a movie."

"Hey, don't bother with the forms. I can do them. You just go and have a fun time. Tell Eric I said hi."

"Thank you." Julie smiled. "Goodnight, Travis. Can't believe someone broke one of your records."

"Tell me I can have a redo." Travis smiled.

"You got it." Grinning, Julie hurried down the hallway.

Claire continued toward the storage room and unlocked

a cubby where she inserted the device and secured the door again. "Let's make sure the door locks too."

In the hallway, she double-checked it and then led him toward her office. "I'm glad we didn't find any additional cameras, but having even one in here is still freaking me out."

"Understandable." Travis waited by the door as she gathered items into a leather satchel. "There were no pics from in your house, but we should still do a sweep to check."

Her hand stilled midair, folder clutched tightly, eyes widening. "You think it's possible he planted them there too?"

Travis had scared her again. Not good. "Not likely, but anything's possible and it's best to check."

She inserted the folder. "Then let's get going so we can do that before dinner, and we can relax a bit."

Relax? Was she kidding? Travis wouldn't relax until she had her prototype in hand and her stalker was locked behind bars.

14

Transport was a big deal. Much bigger than Claire anticipated. Coop sat behind the wheel of an SUV that he'd parked by the curb. An SUV was parked in front and another behind him. Gage stood by the building. Jackson halfway to Coop's SUV.

Travis rested his hand on the door. "I'll step out first. Confirm with Gage that we're good to go. Then you move as fast as you can into the back of Coop's vehicle. I'll be right beside you. Once we're securely inside, Gage and Jackson will get into their SUVs."

"Why three vehicles?" she asked.

"The others will have our backs, and we'll want a rescue vehicle in case anything goes wrong."

She looked deep into his eyes to gauge his mood. Concerned. Worried even. "You don't think anything bad will happen though, right?"

"I don't know, and when I don't know, I plan accordingly."

"You're scaring me." She shifted the strap of her satchel on her shoulder, clutching it tight to keep from fidgeting.

"Don't be." He cupped her elbow and squeezed. "We run

these details all the time for high-value political figures. You have the greatest value to me of anyone I've protected, and I won't let anything happen to you. Ever."

Her heart melted into a big old pile of mush. His protection meant the world to her, but his reasoning for it, even more. "It's a good thing Gage and his guys are waiting for us."

"Why's that?"

"I would be kissing you right now."

He groaned. "Please tell me how it's a good thing you're not."

"A discussion for another time." She nodded at Gage, who was giving them a pointed look.

"Okay, forget about kissing and get your head in protection mode. Release that shoulder strap and keep your hands available." Gone was the warm, flirty guy from a moment ago to be replaced by a hard-as-nails operator. "Ready?"

She had to admit to finding both sides of this fine man equally as attractive. But she had to focus. She released the straps and let her hands hang free. "Ready."

He pushed the door open and held up his hand. "Wait here for a second." He stepped over to Gage. They had a brief conversation, and then Travis took an earbud from Gage and put it in his ear. He returned to her. "We're good to go."

She stepped into the sultry night. She'd lived in Orlando for six years now, moving here from Pittsburgh after obtaining her PhD in Human-Computer Interaction from Carnegie Mellon University, and still couldn't get used to the summer weather. She would leave again when this project concluded in a couple of years, but where she would go would depend on the open jobs in her field.

She slid into the vehicle, and Travis fairly hurled himself

in behind her and slammed the door. Gage and Jackson didn't waste a beat but raced to their SUVs.

"Buckle up," Travis said as he grabbed his strap from the sidewall.

Her brain complied, sending a signal to her hands, but they shook, and she fumbled. She might've been joking about kissing Travis, but a good kiss right about now would end these jitters. Still, it would likely replace them with jitters of another kind. She got the clip into the buckle and the sharp click signaled to everyone that she was ready to depart.

Travis pressed his earbud that Gage had given him earlier, then said, "We're good to go."

Gage took off in the lead vehicle, Coop on his heels, then Jackson. They had to wind around the building to the front gate, where Gage stopped and jerked a thumb back at her vehicle as he talked to the guard.

She started to lower her window.

"No," Travis said. "We had Colonel Lynch arrange for an easy exit."

She glanced at him. "Is there anything you guys didn't think of?"

"If so, I can't imagine what it could be." Travis leaned forward. "What about you, Coop? Think we forgot anything."

"No."

She was starting to think Coop would be a one-word guy if given a chance. Gage's SUV took off, and Coop moved forward without stopping by the guard. She glanced over her shoulder. The gate remained upright long enough for Jackson to exit and then it soundly fell.

The drive turned out to be uneventful. Travis's and Coop's constant checking around for any threat was the only action. She'd always been impressed with Travis's skills, but she could now see the Blackwell Tactical team was trained at the same level.

At her house, she remained in the vehicle with Coop and Travis while Gage and Jackson entered her house. Gage carried a small plastic case, but she had no idea what it contained. She did know they were making sure her house was safe for her to enter.

Her house. Safe? Would she ever be able to come here and not remember this ordeal? She would hate to have to move as finding a good rental house was hard, but if that was what stood between her and peace of mind, she would risk the change.

As she waited, she bounced her knee and couldn't seem to stop.

Travis gently rested his hand on it, and she glanced at him.

"You're safe." His firm tone was comforting but didn't do much to ease her stress. Even with these guys surrounding her, she didn't feel completely safe. They were doing their very best for her, but human best might not be enough. Only God could protect them fully.

Oh, please. If You're listening, please keep everyone safe.

Gage and Jackson soon came out. Gage pressed his earbud, and his lips moved.

"We're clear," Travis said.

Coop killed the engine and got out.

"Wait here until I open your door." Travis slipped out and came around to her door. He stood at the ready while Jackson moved halfway down her sidewalk, and Gage remained near the door. A wall of protection.

"We'll reverse procedures from exiting your office building." Travis quickly whisked her into the house, and the men filed in behind her before securing the door.

"First task," Travis said to the men. "We look for hidden cameras."

"I'll get out the scanners," Gage opened the small case he'd carried in and handed out small, black, handheld devices to each guy.

"We picked these up when we went to check out the hotel." Travis turned his on and looked at her. "They'll scan for hidden cameras and make the job go faster."

"Let's do this room first," Gage said. "Then Claire can relax while we scan the other rooms."

As if they'd worked together for years, they moved into action. Splitting up and choosing a wall to scan. Objects like pictures, drapery finials, etc., got a thorough check. Places she would never consider checking. One by one they pronounced the room clear.

She let out a breath and fell onto the sofa. The tension in her body almost too much to bear. But she had to, didn't she? This wasn't over. Not by a long shot.

Travis took Claire's bedroom. He wanted to stay with her, but even more, he didn't like the fact that any guy, even Gage or his men, would search such a private space. Man, he had it bad, and it was time to admit to himself that he didn't care if she'd bailed on him before. He'd never stopped loving her, and their time together proved that. But what he did next? He had no idea.

He ran the scanner over the front of a dresser seated under two large landscape pictures in soothing sunset colors. Good thing they were able to buy the scanners locally so none of them had to paw through her things. He didn't think he could invade her privacy like that.

A bone-chilling scream filled the house.

He dropped the scanner, lifted his sidearm, and charged to the living room.

Claire stood on her sofa, her terrified eyes fixed on a basket sitting on the floor. The lid had been removed and was lying beside the basket. The other guys raced into the room and paused to assess as Travis had done.

She lifted a trembling hand to point. "Snake. In the basket. Coral. Poisonous."

"I've got it," Travis said.

He started to move closer.

"No! Please," she shouted. "It'll strike and they're deadly."

"Don't worry. It's not my first snake rodeo." He chuckled to relieve some of her tension. "We've all been here and handled our share of slimy creatures."

"I don't know." She bit her lip.

"Trust me." He smiled again but kept his gaze pinned to the snake. "I got this."

He got a good look at the snake coiled in the basket. She was right. The thin body had smooth, shiny scales, looking highly polished. That along with the yellow, black, and red rings circling the body were all telltale signs of a coral snake. The blunt and rounded head was pointed at Claire, waiting to strike if needed.

Travis had to be careful. Put a lid on the basket. Not the lid lying next to it. It would take too much time to pick it up and move it to cover the snake. The reptile could strike in that amount of time. Travis had to approach from behind.

He stopped near the television to grab a picture book large enough to cover the basket and moved forward as silently and slowly as he could. *Moving like pond water.* He still remembered the first time his drill sergeant used that term, but he'd also heard it often enough directed at others during his years in the service. Not a term of endearment for sure.

He reached the basket. Lunged with the book. Contained the snake.

Claire dropped like a person taken out by sniper fire. Gage came forward. Placed his hand on the book and nodded at Claire.

Travis joined her on the sofa. She was crying now, her whole body shaking.

Gage lifted the basket and looked at his men. "Let's get this thing outside. Call animal control and sweep the area."

Travis appreciated Gage taking charge, as it gave him alone time with Claire to comfort her in private.

He pinned his gaze to Gage. "Make arrangements."

Only two words, but Gage nodded his understanding. They needed to find another place for Claire to live for the time being. A place they could rent under a name not connected to Claire in any way. Then they would have to change up Claire's transport. Use a decoy method. Send multiple vehicles out any time they transported her to confuse the suspect.

Claire's crying ramped up, the sobs tearing at his heart. He should resist touching her. Too bad. He couldn't. He swiveled and drew her into his arms. Her body convulsed under his hold, and he tightened his arms.

"Shh, honey." He stroked her back.

Her crying continued, and just when he lost hope of her calming down, the sobs seemed to reach a pinnacle and then slowed.

"That's it," he whispered. "Everything's okay."

She leaned back to grab a piece of paper from the sofa. "N-n-no. It's not. This was on top of the basket." She sniffled and handed the paper to him. "That's why I opened it in the first place."

Travis read the typed message.

I've proved I can get to you, and I want the specs for the software tomorrow. Don't make me escalate my efforts. Watch your phone if you value your life. I'll be in touch.

So their bad guy had come crawling out of the woodwork.

"I can't stay here," she said. "Not after this."

"I wouldn't let you, anyway." Holding the paper felt like fire in his hands so he set it down. "Gage is already making arrangements for an alternate home for you."

"But where?"

"Likely a hotel, but maybe a house rental. Depends on what he thinks we can defend best."

She swiped away tears on her cheeks, leaving her glasses askew. "This is just getting way out of control. I'm not sure I can handle it."

"You're a strong woman, Claire. Stronger than you give yourself credit for. You'll get through it. God is with you, and I'll help in any way I can."

Starting with finding the creep who'd now played his hand. A good thing as far as Travis was concerned. He was skilled at smoking out hidden enemies, but he was even better at crushing ones who'd surfaced.

Four hours later, in Claire's garage, she climbed into Jackson's vehicle along with Travis to go to her temporary hotel. They might be in the vehicle but they had to lie on the floor so they weren't visible. The team had taken turns backing their SUVs into the garage and then leaving. If the suspect was watching them, he wouldn't know which SUV she'd gotten into. Still, Jackson would take a circuitous route to be sure they weren't followed.

Pretty ingenious if you asked her. But then these guys handled protection details all the time and were very resourceful. She couldn't be in better hands.

The tires rolled over the road, and she lay there wishing Travis were in the same seat as her. His warmth telling her he was close by and ready to help her if needed. But they both wouldn't fit comfortably for the thirty-minute drive to the posh hotel, so he took the floor behind her.

She'd never stayed in a five-star hotel, but Gage had chosen it for a few reasons. The staff accommodated their special needs and it had a top-floor suite with an elevator entrance restricted to the key card holder. Plus, at the cost of this suite, he didn't believe the suspect would think they would stay there.

She'd attended a wedding at this hotel, so even though she couldn't see the place when they arrived, she could visualize the entrance. The tall columns. The wide mahogany doors. The bellhops ready to take luggage to rooms and park fancy cars. To make their guests feel special and important.

Not that they went in that way. No, they parked at the loading dock, and the team hustled her into the service elevator. The space was tight with all four men and her, but it whisked them to the eleventh floor. She adjusted the big scarf and dark glasses Travis had her wear to hide her identity. Gage had told the manager that she was a celebrity whose name they wouldn't share, and that she needed her privacy.

She felt like one. Like royalty with the men escorting her. Or the president with his secret service detail. Though he would have far more protection and an advance team. Once the room was found, Gage and Coop had come over to check it out and make arrangements before booking. So she had her own advance team of sorts.

Gage and Coop stepped out, hands on the butts of their guns.

Gage nodded. "Door's not more than fifty feet down a private hall. Follow us."

Coop strode off over the plush paisley-patterned carpet. Gage behind. Claire followed them. Travis walked beside her, and Jackson brought up the rear. She nearly had to run to keep up with their pace. Despite the danger, she wanted to laugh at being a security detail sandwich.

Coop stopped at her suite with a gleaming mahogany door and used his key card to release the lock. He and Gage disappeared inside, and she waited with Travis and Jackson. Her smile evaporated. This wasn't a casual outing. It was serious. Her foe had announced his intention to hurt her if she didn't give him the information he wanted, and she wasn't about to hand it over.

Gage poked his head out. "We're clear."

She entered, followed by Travis and Jackson, who let out a low whistle. "Now this is what I call a suite."

As did Claire. Floor-to-ceiling windows in a massive sitting room with velvet sofas and polished walnut tables overlooked the city skyline. Both sides of the room were lined with doors leading to three bedrooms.

"Let's get those blinds closed," Travis said.

Coop went to the window to draw them.

Travis turned to her. "Even with them closed and being on such a high floor, I want you to stay away from the windows."

"Okay," she said, fighting a shiver at his intensity.

He planted his hands on his hips and widened his stance. "And it goes without saying that you do not leave the room without us."

"Wouldn't dream of it," she said, but then wondered if

she might indeed dream about it tonight. A nightmare for sure.

"Your bedroom is on that side." Gage pointed to the left. "My team will share the bedrooms on the right."

"Right now, I want someone on duty outside the door," Travis said.

Gage nodded. "Coop and Jackson are still on Portland time so they'll take the first shifts while I get some shuteye."

"Good." Travis gave his buddy a tight nod.

The men took off as if they'd already talked about leaving her alone with Travis to get acclimated to her new home.

"I'll head to the lobby to get Eryn when she arrives." Gage went to one bedroom.

Coop and Jackson started for the front door. Coop peered over his shoulder. "I'll grab the luggage from the vehicle and then park it in the garage."

"And I'll stand duty," Jackson said.

They stepped out the door, and just like that she was alone with Travis. Nervous now for some reason, she looked around until she spotted a small kitchenette. She looked in the refrigerator and found bottled water. She took one out and held it up. "Want one?"

"Sure."

She grabbed another bottle and sat on the sofa.

"You should probably be getting some shuteye too."

"I want to meet Eryn when she gets here and see if she found anything of interest in the network."

Travis checked his watch. "Her plane's on the ground, and she should be here soon. Until then, let's review the security protocol again. I'll be spending the night in this room. We'll have someone outside the suite door at all times. If our suspect gets past them and me, you'll have two guys and Eryn in the other rooms who'll come running. But if for some reason I'm incapacitated, I want you to call 911 and request a patrol officer."

"You think he can get past you?" She pushed her glasses higher on her nose and didn't like that she was showing her fear.

"Not at all. The odds of taking out four spec ops guys and a former FBI agent are low. Just covering all bases. I won't leave anything to chance when it comes to your safety." His intensity had disappeared to be replaced with a tender, soft gaze that wrapped her in the warmth of his caring.

Oh, gosh. She was lost. Totally lost. And in love again. No, not again. Still. He was the man for her. The *only* man, and she had to face that fact. So either she lived a life of loneliness or she got used to dealing with her fear of losing him.

Which would it be?

∿

Eryn was not at all what Claire had expected. She had to admit to having a stereotypical picture of her looking like a tough law enforcement officer. But she didn't come across that way at all. She was around five foot seven with a curvy figure, long dark hair, and a pleasant smile. However, her attire told of her former occupation as she wore black tactical pants and a red polo shirt with a gun at her hip almost hidden under an overshirt.

After introductions were complete, she dropped her computer case on the second sofa across from the one Claire sat on with Travis. "I got in right away and had a chance to look around. I was onto something when I got kicked off the network. I think we could be looking at White for this."

Claire sat forward. "But he's out of town."

"Or so he says." Eryn gave a proud smile. "Checked his credit card, and he's holed up in a dumpy motel down the road."

"He's what?" Claire jumped to her feet and started pacing. "He lied to us?"

"About where he is, yes," Eryn said. "I'll need to get into the network to investigate my theory before we can prove he lied about other things and go after him."

Claire stopped pacing. "Let's go then. Now!"

"Not a good idea," Travis said. "Everyone needs to get some shuteye so we're better prepared for what we might face tomorrow. Especially now that we could be hauling this guy in. We need to bring our A game."

He was right, but... "Like I can sleep anyway."

"Trust me," Eryn said. "You might toss and turn, but the guys can sleep through anything."

"And you?"

"I'm a mom. I don't sleep through anything." She laughed.

Claire had forgotten that Eryn was a mother. "I'm sorry about taking you away from your child."

"Bekah loves it when I go out of town. My mom takes care of her and spoils her rotten."

Gage had told them that Eryn's husband had died, and she was raising their daughter on her own. Took a strong woman to be a successful single parent, and Claire admired Eryn even though she didn't know her.

Claire would ask more about Bekah later, right now she wanted to talk about Warren's guilt. She couldn't wait to look him in the eye. To read him the riot act. Such betrayal. From one of the people closest to her at work. The one in charge of security. The one she'd trusted to keep her pet project safe.

Grr. She was vibrating with anger.

Claire shook her head and kept shaking it. "I still can't believe it could be Warren, but then it makes sense as he knows a lot about my private life and could invade my home. But what about Mike and those pictures?"

"Looks like he might just be your garden variety stalker with a romantic interest in you," Eryn said.

"Interest!" Travis grunted. "That goes beyond interest to obsession. And he'll need to be called to account for the hidden camera."

"We have to prove it was him first," Eryn said. "I can look at the camera in the morning. See how he was getting his feed."

Travis nodded. "So what say those of us who are turning in do so? We'll start tomorrow by going to the hotel for Claire's appointment then get to the office and prove that Robb was stalking her and Warren White is the guy behind the thefts. Then we'll raid his hotel room and hold him for the police to haul off to jail."

A big day. A very big day. And Claire would be right there. No matter what Travis said. Oh, he would argue the point all right. But she would prevail. Sleep or no sleep tonight, she would be ready to let Warren have it and watch with satisfaction as he was hauled off to jail in the back seat of a police car.

15

Why had Travis agreed to this hotel visit? Just a thirty-minute detour, but it stopped them from getting to the network. Still, he promised to take her if it was safe to do so, and he was a man of his word.

He got out of the punishing sunshine and slid behind Eryn in the cool vehicle she'd rented at the airport. Travis wasn't sure about her driving with a bum hand, but Gage vouched for her. And the big bonus was if their suspect was lying in wait, he wouldn't have seen her vehicle or associated a woman with Claire's protection team.

"Approaching the hotel loading dock now," Eryn said.

She parked, and Gage, Jackson, and Coop soon joined them to escort Claire safely inside. They took watch at the doors, and Travis kept Claire by his side as he waited in the small ballroom for the event coordinator to get there. Eric and Julie had arrived several minutes before to stroll off arm-in-arm to look at the room, and as Eric had said, "Assess the acoustics."

Claire had watched them, the longing in her eyes unmistakable. Despite her comments about a relationship, he knew she really did want someone in her life, though he doubted she'd accepted that yet.

She shivered violently and ran her hands over her arms.

"I'd have thought after growing up in the north that the frigid temperatures they keep this place would seem like beach weather to you," he teased.

She cast him a playful grin. "That was before I moved to Orlando and acclimated to the sweltering summer temperatures. Now I get cold when it drops to the sixties."

"Lightweight." He pulled her under his arm for warmth. *Yeah, right. For warmth.*

She rested her head on his chest. His heart thundered. She was the only woman who'd brought such life to his day. But did she reciprocate or was she just letting her jealousy over Julie and Eric get to her?

Michelle, a slight redhead with hair pulled up and wearing a professional navy suit, entered the room. She carried a clipboard and wore an intensity on her face that Travis appreciated. Much more intense today and less of yesterday's flirty behavior.

Claire slipped free, her all-business expression leaving no doubt that she'd moved on from the special moment with him. Maybe only special to him.

The coordinator approached, a large padded envelope resting on her clipboard. "You people really do take your security seriously."

"Military protocol," Travis said, trying to play it down.

"Well, I can assure you that we will abide by your request to have you screen arriving guests and our workers as they deliver food and drinks."

Claire smiled at the woman. "We appreciate your cooperation."

"Of course. I know how important this event is to you

and no one will disturb it." She held the envelope out to Claire. "This was left at the front desk for you this morning."

"For me? Here?" Claire reached out for the package.

Travis intercepted the package, but made sure to hold it by the corner to limit adding his fingerprints to the surface. "Any idea who left it?"

"No," Michelle said.

"You have a security camera at the front desk, right?" Travis asked. "So we could look at the footage and see who dropped it off."

"I suppose you could." She smoothed a hand over her hair. "If my manager agrees."

"Can you arrange that for us?"

"I'll ask him when we finish here."

Travis held up the envelope and looked at Claire. "Let's wait to open this until later."

Claire blinked, seeming to grasp the risks of what the envelope might contain.

"I'll just give it to Gage to hold onto." Travis strode to the door when he wanted to run. Gage stood duty just outside.

"This was left at the front desk for Claire. Doubt it's a good thing." Travis handed over the envelope.

Gage took it by the same corner without needing to be told. "Any idea who left it?"

"No, but I've arranged for the coordinator to help us get a look at the security video when Claire is done here."

"If that doesn't show us anything, we'll need to get this processed for fingerprints."

"Too bad Sierra isn't still here."

Gage nodded. "We could get it X-rayed. That way we preserve the evidence, and yet, know what the envelope contains."

"Great idea," Travis said, mulling it over. "I can't see a doctor's office or hospital agreeing to that."

Gage stared at the package. "What about a vet's office? They might."

"We'd have a better chance there, but Claire doesn't have a pet, and I doubt she has that kind of connection."

"Maybe someone she works with does."

"I'll ask her and Julie if they know someone. Until then, get one of your men to take this to the vehicle for safe-keeping."

"Roger that."

Travis went back into the room where Claire, Julie, and Eric were discussing the equipment that would be provided for the music. Eric, who'd seemed low-key, was animated as he talked about DJing the party. Could be he liked to live a little after his desk job. Travis had checked the guy out before letting him attend today's meeting and learned that Eric came from a prominent, wealthy local family and was employed at a big retailer as a cloud solutions architect. A linear thinker like most IT people and not the kind of guy Travis would expect to become a DJ or a competitive body-builder, but he was both.

Travis stood back during the planning meeting, chiming in only when security-related items came up. Thankfully, it was all over in the thirty minutes he'd allotted, even with Michelle's flirty behavior.

She started to walk away.

"You'll check on that security video for us?" Travis asked.

"Right away, then I'll meet you at the front desk." She took off, her high heels clicking on the parquet flooring.

As they headed for the door, he looked at the group. "Anyone know a vet who might be willing to X-ray a package Claire received?"

"My dog's vet is very accommodating," Eric said. "He's been our family vet for as long as I can remember, and he's just down the road. I can give him a call. I'm sure he'll do it if I ask."

"Make the call," Travis said and stopped walking so they could arrange this X-ray before they departed.

Julie looked at him. "Why do you want the package X-rayed?"

"Could be from Claire's stalker, and we want to see what it contains before we open it. Just to be safe."

"Shouldn't you just give it to the police?" Julie asked.

She was asking good questions. Ones that Travis didn't want to answer, but he also didn't want to raise her suspicions by being evasive. "We will, but they're not so good at sharing and we need to know what it contains to make sure Claire is safe."

Julie rested her hand on Claire's shoulder. "It just plain stinks that you have a stalker. I wish I could do something to help find this guy."

"There's nothing you can do." Claire gave her friend a wobbly smile. "But thanks for your support. That means a lot."

Travis tuned them out to listen to Eric's conversation. He handled the vet like a man of privilege who was used to others doing his bidding. Didn't seem to be the kind of guy who would date Julie, someone he or his family might perceive as beneath him. But then he was clearly in love and love didn't look at social standing. Love just happened. No matter if you were trying to stop it. Travis knew that better than many men.

Eric shoved his phone into the pocket of his dress slacks. "We're good to go. You can follow me to the office."

"Hey, thanks, man," Travis said.

"Claire's Julie's friend and I want Julie to be happy so..." He shrugged.

"Then let's go. I need to make a quick stop at the front

desk. Go ahead and pull your car out front, and we'll follow you."

Eric strode over to Julie and took her hand. "My vet agreed so let's go."

"Thank you, Eric," Claire said.

"No worries. You know I'm always glad to help." He led Julie to the door.

"Is that true?" Travis asked Claire. "*Is* he always glad to help? I got the feeling on his phone call that he's used to being catered to."

"He's a great guy. Most of the time you'd never know he had prominent parents who no one says no to. There are moments when it comes out, but for the most part, he's just a regular guy and I like him."

"I suppose it would be hard to fully eliminate something you were born into." Travis gestured at the door. "We should get going. We'll stop at the front desk and hopefully get the video."

Claire's phone rang. "It's Michelle."

Claire answered and put her on speaker. "Sorry, Claire. My manager said he's not allowed to release any video except to law enforcement if they have a warrant."

The answer Travis expected, but didn't like. But he wouldn't give up. He wouldn't leave Claire's side, and there was no reason to take Claire to the lobby just to get the manager's information for the call Travis intended to make to plead their case. "Could you give us his contact information so we can follow up with him?"

"I can text it to you."

"Perfect," Travis said. "Thank you."

"Of course." Michelle ended the call.

"Let's get out of here." Travis took Claire's elbow and moved her toward the door. "I'll have Gage circle back to talk to him. I'm sure he'll be more persuasive."

They exited and used transport protocol, whisking Claire into the vehicle, then following Eric and Julie to a small vet's practice on a side street a few blocks away.

Gage hopped out with the envelope to join Eric, and they disappeared inside.

Eryn tapped her finger on the wheel, likely eager to get to the office and start her network search. Travis was eager for that to happen too, but this envelope could be their best lead yet. And, of course, keeping Claire safe in this lot and transporting her was top priority now.

Gage came marching out of the office with the package and headed straight for Eryn's SUV. Travis lowered his window.

Eric hurried to keep up with Gage but he turned to him. "Thanks for your help. If you want to get back to work, we'd be glad to drive Julie to the institute since that's where we're headed."

"Hey, thanks, man," Eric said. "That would be great, but what's in there anyway?"

"I'm not at liberty to say." Gage cast him a tight smile. "Like I said. Thanks for the help. We appreciate it. If you'll send Julie over, we'll get going."

"Anytime." Eric went to his gleaming silver Porsche, where Julie waited for him.

Gage approached the window. "Envelope contains a typed letter to Claire with a picture of Julie. Basically, it says if Claire won't consider her own safety, she should consider Julie's as she's completely disposable."

Claire gasped. "That's why you offered to drive her to work."

Gage nodded. "We'll need to read her in and bring her to the hotel with us today."

Claire clasped her hands in her lap. "I hate that I put her in danger."

"You didn't do anything," Travis said. "Our thief did."

Julie got out of the car, and Claire's focus locked on her friend.

"We'll drop this conversation for now and hold off telling her until we can strategize and get my CO's approval," Travis said. "Agreed?"

"Agreed," Gage said.

Claire kept watching her friend and absently nodded.

Gage opened the back door for Julie.

"Thanks, guys," she said. "Eric hates to miss work and let his colleagues down, so it's good for him to get back sooner rather than later."

Travis looked over the seat at the pair. Claire smiled at her friend, but guilt consumed Claire's face. Thankfully, Julie was looking out the window at Eric as he peeled out of the lot and didn't catch Claire's look.

"And he loves his car." Julie laughed.

Claire joined in, and for a brief moment he saw the happy woman who he'd worked alongside to create CATS.

Eryn got them on the road, taking all of Travis's attention. Thankfully, Claire talked to Julie about recent simulation test results and what they needed to schedule in the next few days.

"You have plans tonight?" Claire asked.

"Other than working late, no. I'm running behind and after everything you just mentioned, I have a full plate." She chuckled.

Travis liked Julie's easygoing nature and how much she cared for Claire. That proximity to Claire putting Julie in serious danger. Travis hated that. Hated seeing another woman targeted for death. He would do all he could to protect her.

Eryn turned onto the institute's drive. "Whoa."

Travis's pulse kicked into gear, and he scanned ahead.

The overflow parking lot was filled with rows and rows of vases holding vibrant red roses, slightly wilting in the hard beating sun.

Odd. Roses, why?

On the far side of the lot, a man dressed in a black tuxedo had his back to them as he attached a vinyl banner to the fence. He glanced furtively over his shoulder, then turned back to his work.

"It's Robb," Travis said.

"Mike?" Claire asked and leaned forward. "What in the world is he up to?"

"Whatever it is, you stay out of sight while I check it out." Travis reminded Eryn that Robb could be Claire's stalker. "He could be dangerous. React accordingly."

"Roger that." Eryn reached for her sidearm.

Travis waited for Claire to duck down, then grabbed his door handle, letting in a wash of air.

Claire had risen up and looked over the seat at him. "Be careful, okay?"

"Hey," he said, making sure to lighten his tone. "Don't worry. I'm trained to handle myself in dangerous circumstances."

"Still." She held his gaze. "Be careful. For me."

"Of course."

He may have played down this situation for Claire, but as he jogged across the road, he kept his hand firmly seated on his gun. The biggest mistake he could make would be to underestimate his enemy, and Robb was the enemy until proven otherwise.

Travis stealthily moved in. Five feet from his target, he cleared his throat. "Hello, Robb."

Robb spun. His gaze quickly ran over Travis then took in Eryn's rental vehicle.

With a big smile, Robb started for the road.

For Claire.

Had Robb seen Claire? Figured she was in the car?

Robb slipped his hand into his coat pocket.

Gun! Travis reacted on instinct, bolting after Robb and tackling him to the ground. He straddled his back.

"What the—?" Robb mumbled as he squirmed. "What're you doing, man, and what's my girl doing in your car?"

Travis slowly turned Robb over and jerked his hand out of the pocket. A black velvet box lay in his palm. A ring? He was going to ask Claire to marry him?

"This is your grand gesture?" Travis stifled a burst of hysterical laughter threatening to escape. "Flowers and a proposal?"

Robb's eyes narrowed. "What business is it of yours? And I'll ask again, what're you doing with Claire?"

"I'm doing some testing for the Army while I'm in town, and she's working on the project."

"You didn't mention that the other night."

Travis released Robb's wrist and stood, keeping his hand on his gun just in case Robb tried anything. "What are the odds that the Claire I work with and the Claire you mentioned are the same person?"

"Fair enough, but what's with the tackle?" Robb tried to scoot back.

Travis held firm. "Someone attacked Claire the other day. I thought you might have a gun."

"Me?" Robb's mouth dropped open. "I'd never hurt Claire. I love her and have to ask her to marry me."

Travis eyed the guy, putting a healthy measure of warning in his gaze. "Trust me. She's not available. Especially not to a stalker like you."

Travis hauled Robb past Eryn's vehicle to Gage, who'd pulled up behind and was out with his eye on them. Travis wanted to question him about the attack but he was so angry right now he could do something he would regret. Better to put distance between them until he cooled down.

"Take this guy." Travis patted Robb down for any additional weapons then opened the back door of Gage's SUV to shove Robb inside and slam the door, letting all his frustration with the stalker into the effort. "I need your guys to detain him, and I'll have Eryn work on the camera first thing. Hopefully we'll have something illegal to pin on him and get the police out here to take him into custody."

Gage gave a sharp nod. "I'll have Jackson or Coop park in the lot and wait for word from you."

"Thanks, man." Travis spun and raced back to Claire. He climbed into the front passenger's seat and looked back at her.

"I know," she said before he could get his door closed. "You don't have to say it. I didn't listen. I sat up. I'm sorry, but I wanted to be sure you were okay."

This time it was okay, but… "Promise me you won't go against my directives again."

She nibbled on her lip.

"Please."

"Fine," she finally said. "I promise."

"Good, because I know you would never break your promises."

"Never," she said, but then pressed her lips together.

Okay, fine. She didn't want to promise, but she had, and it could very well be the thing that kept her alive.

"Get us to the front entrance, Eryn," Travis said.

"Roger that." She put the SUV into gear and moved forward.

At the door, Travis, Gage, and Eryn rushed Claire and Julie inside. When Travis took Claire's elbow, he could feel her shaking. He drew her to a stop in a private alcove as the others moved on.

"Claire, honey." He took her chin in his hand and looked into her eyes. "Are you all right?"

She shivered, and he knew it wasn't from the cool building temperature. His gut cramped, and he stepped closer to her, needing to touch her. Maybe as proof that Robb hadn't harmed her.

Not shifting his focus, Travis drew her toward him, giving her every chance to pull away.

Her eyes warmed instead, and he couldn't help himself. He dipped his head and claimed her lips. Soft. Warm. Like he remembered. He put his heart and soul into the kiss, making sure she knew how he felt. She returned it ounce-for-ounce. The unexpected passion he remembered from the usually serious woman.

He wanted to simply enjoy it, but was she responding to him now out of love or just a need for connection after a frightening event? He knew that he loved her...but could he trust her to love him back? Could he give her the power to break his heart again?

Would they have a chance to find out?

Because before they could ever have a second chance together, he needed to make sure her tenacious attacker didn't lay his hands on her ever again.

16

Standing in the hallway outside her office with Gage, Julie, and Travis, Claire could still feel the tingle of his lips on hers. She wished they were still kissing. The intensity of her emotions shocked her. She couldn't believe the sense of belonging and oneness with Travis that she'd always felt with him. And she wanted more. Much more.

Enough to let go of her fear? To trust that even if she got hurt again, God would get her through it?

"Claire," Travis said, drawing her back. "You said no one knew about the meeting with the coordinator, so do you have any idea how this creep knew to deliver that envelope to the hotel?"

"No," she said, trying to concentrate on anything other than how full his lips were. "I didn't tell anyone other than Julie and Eric. But a lot of people know about the party tomorrow so maybe it was left for me to get tomorrow."

"Claire...I..." Julie wrung her hands. "I mentioned it to a few people here. But that was okay, right? I mean, Robb's likely your stalker and the guy who attacked you, and he doesn't work at the institute now."

"Let's talk about this later," Claire said before Julie asked additional questions, and Claire was forced to lie to her friend. "For now, we need to get to work."

"I'll meet you in your office," Gage said and took off in that direction.

"I have a development meeting I'm late for anyway." Julie's eyes narrowed in the way they did when Claire had crushed her friend's feelings. Julie was easy going most of the time, but she was also very sensitive.

Claire wanted to explain, but she had to let it go. "See you later."

Once Julie had marched down the hallway, Claire faced Travis. "You have to convince your CO to let us tell Julie what's going on."

"I'll call him as soon as I can, but don't be surprised if he says no."

"How can he when she's confused and suffering and maybe another target?"

"She really has no reason to know other than not to ruin your friendship and that doesn't trump national security."

Okay, so she didn't like his answer but she could see it. And he was willing to ask even if he thought he would be shot down. Surprised at his easy acquiescence on the matter, she continued to watch him. Or maybe she just wanted to watch him. Maybe touch him. Experience the warmth between them again.

He arched an eyebrow. "What's with the look?"

"I didn't think you would agree to ask your CO so quickly."

"Despite what most women think, men aren't oblivious to everything. I saw how upset Julie was, and I'll help if I can."

"Thank you." His kindness had always been something she'd admired, adding another check mark in a column that had filled fast in his favor.

He didn't say anything else. Maybe he was replaying the incident and trying to figure out their next move. Or maybe he was thinking about the kiss that told her he still had feelings for her. Deep feelings like the ones she was experiencing.

Was she foolish for shutting him out?

A vision of Travis hitting his head and losing consciousness in the attack at her home flashed before her eyes. Even in a sleepy suburb of Orlando, Travis could've been killed in the blink of an eye.

How ironic. She'd chosen not to get involved with him because of the dangers of his job in foreign countries, but danger lurked all around all the time. Car accidents. Burning houses. Plane crashes. He could die anywhere. Anytime. His job increased the odds, but no job existed that would leave him completely safe. At least not a job that he would do.

She looked at him, and for the first time in two years, she let her feelings for him run free. Her heart was full and whole as she was sure God intended for her. She wanted to embrace the emotions. Be happy. Be content, but she couldn't change years of running from pain in an instant—if she could change at all. Once they wrapped all of this up, she would take the time for some intense thinking.

Eryn poked her head around the corner. "We should get started."

"Yes, right." Claire got Eryn set up on the small table in the corner where Gage was sitting and looking at his phone.

"I'm going to the conference room to have a private conversation with my CO," Travis said.

Claire nodded and wished she could listen in to his conversation, but he deserved privacy. Besides, the room where Mike had hidden a camera brought back his altercation with Travis and all she could think about was sitting up to check on them and then seeing the incident. Travis's quick reflexes impressed her. She'd seen them in the simulations, but it was even more impressive in real life, taking Mike down like he was a scarecrow not a guy who worked out.

Mike. Man. He had to be delusional, planning to propose to her after stalking her. She wouldn't be comfortable again until he was arrested. But how long of a sentence would a guy get for putting a camera in her office and stalking her? Probably not long enough. Hopefully, at least the two years she needed to finish this project and could move elsewhere.

First, they had to make the camera charges stick. She and Gage watched as Eryn connected the camera to her computer and her fingers flew over the keyboard. She glanced up every now and then and frowned at them.

"Isn't there something you two could do other than stare at me?" she asked.

"Gage and Travis could run a scenario or two on the simulator," Claire suggested.

"Thanks. I can work faster with you out of my hair." Eryn didn't take her eyes from the screen.

"Text if you need us," Gage said.

Her only acknowledgment was a flick of her fingers. Just like Nick, she was fully engaged in her work.

They entered the hallway to find Travis on his way back. He shook his head, the result Claire had expected.

She smiled to ease his frustration. "I have a two-man cave scenario that you can put your frustration into."

Travis grinned. "I'd be all over that."

She got the devices from the storage room and gave them to the guys in the simulator room.

"Gage, yours is an outdated version since one of the

current ones was stolen," she said. "Give me a second to update it with new firmware, and we'll get going."

"Yeah, man," Travis said. "Outdated, just like you."

Gage socked Travis in the arm. "See if I have your back in the simulation."

"You will. You always do."

Claire liked the confidence in Travis's voice as she went to the observation room and loaded the updated program. Her dad never really talked about having the backs of other soldiers, but he demonstrated it as did his buddies when they came to the house or she went to parties they held. She remembered as a kid being jealous of his army teammates. Her dad had a family in them. A family she couldn't be a part of.

The same kind of family Travis would have to be forced to leave. More than forced. Maybe pried away from. He had a connection deeper than her father's and that had been strong.

The computer dinged the update conclusion. She pressed the mic. "You guys ready to go?"

"I am," Gage said, his virtual device still hanging from his hand. "But this guy is gonna have to book it to keep up with me."

Travis grinned and settled his virtual device over his eyes. "We'll see who's trying to keep up."

They laughed together and assumed the start position. She clicked on the program and the deep, dark, and dangerous caves they'd created spread open on the screen.

Thankfully, Julie had that development meeting, so Claire didn't have to stand next to her in the observation room as Travis and Gage ran their scenario. Their virtual personas entered the cave, and Claire shuddered as she could nearly feel the cold and dank real-life scenario.

But the guys didn't stop for anything and moved in

tandem. As one fighting machine. When one failed the other took over and time flew as she watched her baby pushed to the limit. She wished she could film these sessions so Army brass could see Travis in action, not just see his simulation scores. Or maybe she just wanted to watch them after he was gone, leaving her behind.

Don't go there. Keep focused just like they're doing.

An hour into the session, Eryn texted. *Need help.*

Claire paused the scenario and relayed the message to the guys over the speaker. "We have to lock up the devices before we go to the office."

The three of them made quick work of stowing them securely and rushed back to Claire's office.

Eryn tapped the camera sitting on the table. "He recorded video too. Found the files on the server."

Travis glowered at the camera but his gaze quickly brightened. "This is good news."

"What?" Claire gaped at him. "How could Mike recording me be good news?"

"In addition to stalking charges, Robb was eavesdropping on your work environment and that would fall under espionage."

Oh, wow. Wow! That was serious. She doubted that was his intent. So the big question was, could she do that to him, even if he was stalking her? She might not have a choice as the Army brass would determine the charges. "I doubt that was his intent, but it would keep him locked up longer."

Gage moved closer to Eryn. "Is that why you wanted us?"

"No." Eryn leaned back, her fingers still hovering over the trackpad. "I need Robb's phone. But make sure he willingly surrenders it or we won't be able to use it when we approach law enforcement."

"On it." Gage got out his cell and called Jackson to make the request.

"You think he'll give the phone up willingly?" Claire asked.

"Jackson and Coop have very persuasive personalities." Gage chuckled.

As the time ticked past, Claire imagined Coop and Jackson at work persuading Mike to give up what these days was a lifeline to so many people. Still, she'd seen Travis's persuasive techniques in action and knew all operators were trained to get information from uncooperative suspects. Mike really didn't stand a chance.

Her desk phone buzzed. She picked up the call from the reception desk. "A Jackson Lockhart is at the desk for you."

"I'll be right out." Smiling, she eased between Travis and Gage and tried not to run down the hallway and draw her staff's attention even more than the frequent gatherings with the team in her office had probably done.

"Passcode turned off." Jackson handed her the phone and after a quick nod departed.

"I've heard of getting a guy's phone number, but his phone?" Bethany winked.

Claire didn't know how to respond, so she didn't.

"You have to tell me where you're finding all these single hunks." Bethany grinned.

"Just part of the program," Claire said, keeping up her normal professional behavior.

"Okay, I get it. Keep my big mouth shut." Bethany mocked zipping her lips.

"I'll see you later." Claire stepped away. The moment her stalker and their thief was behind bars, she would have a long sit down with her team and explain her anxious behavior of late.

She gave the phone to Eryn who immediately tapped the screen.

Claire sat in her chair. "How long before we might know anything?"

"Minutes." Eryn kept her attention on the phone.

The others watched her, including Claire. The time ticking slowly by. Second by second. One minute. Two. Three. Five.

"Yes." Eryn shot up a fist. "We've got him. Time to call in the police."

"You have concrete proof?" Travis asked.

She nodded. "His phone was used to retrieve the pictures and videos from the server here."

Claire was glad to have this resolved. Extremely glad. Sure she was, but... "Why didn't our network administrator see the outside access?"

"Your team is employing a VPN—virtual private network—usually safe and masks the network for outsiders, but Robb hacked it. He pulled the photos and videos once a week and was moving decent-sized packets of data at a time so it should've triggered alerts unless he hacked those too. I can figure that out, but we've got enough on him for an arrest and I'd like to move on to White."

"We need to consult with the colonel in charge here before calling the police," Gage said.

Eryn looked at him. "If you're okay with Jackson and Coop babysitting Robb a little longer, I'll follow that trail to Warren White, and you can talk to the colonel about both of them to save time."

"Works for me," Gage said.

"I work faster without an audience." She waved over her head. "Go do something, and I'll call the minute I have him."

Claire stood. "We can finish the simulations."

"Another chance to skunk Gage?" Travis pushed off the corner of the desk. "I'm all for that."

Gage rolled his eyes. "In your dreams."

In the hallway, Travis looked at her. "You two go ahead. I need to have a word with Robb."

"Hands off." Gage arched an eyebrow. "You *and* my guys. Tell them that. We don't want the arrest to go south."

"No worries," Travis called back at them but kept walking.

She stared after him. "What's that all about?"

"Robb will likely get bail, so Travis's going to read him the riot act. Tell him to keep away from you."

"And you think Travis might attack him?" She started down the hallway.

Gage stepped beside her. "Attack? No. Place a few mean-ingful punches to get his message across? Yes. But he's not going to do that and neither are my guys."

"But they would have if you hadn't warned Travis?"

"Operators have each other's backs. You hurt someone one of us cares about, you hurt all of us. And if one of us is in need we're there. No questions asked."

"The same way you came here for Travis," she said.

"Yeah, like that, but I did ask a few questions first." He laughed. "Still, whether I liked G-man's answers or not, I would've been here."

She got that part. The good part. Her dad had a similar code. But the ugly part? Threatening and maybe beating someone up for her. That was well out of her normal world. She sure couldn't imagine her dad having done that, but she suspected he would have if called upon.

She wouldn't condone such behavior, but she did like seeing how the guys cared for each other. Even more proof that their team was their family. Something Travis had mentioned a few times even though he had a loving birth family too. Another example of why he would never leave the team to be with her. No, if she wanted to follow these feelings for him, she would have to leave her project behind and move.

And there she had it. She was in the same place as when she'd broken up with him.

Question was, would she react the same way?

∽

Travis had barely begun to read Robb the riot act when he received a group text from Eryn. She'd found something concrete on White already. He left Robb behind and returned to the institute. He'd hopefully proved his point. Jackson and Coop would drill it home too. Robb had seemed properly scared. For now, anyway. But what happened when Travis and the guys went back to their own cities? Robb could easily find out they didn't live here and pick up right where he'd left off.

Travis couldn't let that happen. If Robb got a lenient sentence, Travis wouldn't have any choice on whether he accepted the job Colonel Lynch offered. Travis would be here for Claire.

"Another hot one out there." He smiled at Bethany as he scanned the key card Claire had issued to him.

"And in here too." She used her hand with long blue nails to fan her face.

"I'll have Claire check the air conditioning to be sure it's working correctly." He got her flirting reference, but he wasn't about to encourage it.

"No need." She frowned and turned back to her computer.

Ignoring women who came on to them was one thing Travis and most spec ops guys got used to doing. Something few of them wanted to become pros at doing.

By the time he got to the office, Claire was behind her

desk. Eryn was still sitting at the small round table in the corner, and Gage was with her.

"What took you so long?" Gage asked.

"Had business to finish."

"Let's get down to it," Eryn said. "White accessed the network multiple times in the past week, including the night of the software theft."

"But how do you know?" Claire asked. "He can't be dumb enough to use his own login to steal the software."

"He wasn't," Eryn said. "He hacked the network just like I did by sending a phishing email to your receptionist."

Claire gaped at her. "We teach the staff not to click on those, but then it's up to them."

Eryn nodded. "Don't beat yourself up. I wish I could say it wasn't a common thing, but human error is the biggest factor in network security failure."

"So he got into the network," Travis said. "But not using his own credentials. How do we pin the theft on him?"

"The transmissions tracked to the hotel where he's staying."

"But is that good enough?" Gage asked. "He could claim anyone at the hotel could've accessed the network."

"He could, but he made a big mistake. He used the hotel's guest network, and they will have logs that show access by room. We just need to get a look at those logs."

Claire got up. "Then let's go."

Travis liked her enthusiasm but raised a hand. "Not you. Not only for security reasons, but because White knows you, and if he sees you at the hotel, he'll know we're on to him."

"He could recognize you too from your past trials."

Travis didn't like being left behind, but... "Fair point."

"Time to read Coop and Jackson in on the theft," Gage said. "They need to know what they're facing."

"This is almost over," Travis said. "So no worries."

"Okay, then Eryn can go with Coop to get a look at those network files," Gage said. "He shouldn't recognize either of them. I'll take Coop's place outside with Robb."

"How certain are you that you'll get the information?" Claire asked.

"I don't know the protocol the hotel uses. A reputable hotel will have logs, but this place is a dive and might not care about logging their access for security. So I'd say it's fifty/fifty."

"Not enough for us to get the ball rolling on an arrest with Lynch then?" Claire asked.

"I'd hold off." Eryn stowed her laptop. "Unless you enjoy irritating Army brass."

"I'd rather have a root canal," Claire said.

"Let's split these incidents up so we can move forward with Robb and get him behind bars," Gage said. "Then we'll have the entire team focused on White."

Travis nodded. "We'll go see him, while you hit the hotel. Text us the minute you have proof. Hopefully, we'll still be with Lynch when that happens."

Gage nodded. "I'll get White's room under surveillance while Eryn works on obtaining proof. I'll let you know when I have eyes on him."

They departed, and Travis stood by the door. "Ready? Or should we call ahead?"

"A surprise attack is best." She peered at him in the hallway. "You didn't hurt Mike, did you?"

"Not physically, but emotionally? I sure hope so." She shrunk back. Right. His intensity was likely throwing her for a loop. "Look. I don't condone violence for the most part, but sometimes it's only thing that gets through to men like Robb. Think of me as a deterrent from future offending on his part."

Her lips tipped in a stiff smile. "Thank you for having my back."

"I always will."

"I hope he goes away for at least long enough for me to complete this project. Then if the Army doesn't need me for anything else, I can move and leave Mike behind."

"I don't mean to alarm you," Travis said, though he hated to. "But depending on how infatuated he is, he could still track you down."

Her eyes narrowed. "I might never be free from him?"

"I don't know, but to be safe, you need to consider the possibility."

"I guess you're right, but it's depressing to think I'll have to look over my shoulder for the rest of my life."

"I can help with that."

"How?"

"If the guy gets out of prison or doesn't end up serving time, I can ask Eryn to keep tabs on him, and if he steps out of line, I can have another word with him."

She paused outside Lynch's office door. "You think she could do that for me?"

"I know she can and will if we ask."

"That's comforting." Her worried tone didn't confirm her words.

Travis wanted to promise to move to Florida. To be there for her. By her side. But his throat closed, and he couldn't get the words out. Leaving the team—his family—was a decision he hadn't been able to pull the trigger on, and he apparently wasn't ready to do it now either.

What was it going to take? The woman he now knew he still loved could be in danger, and he was still thinking about his own needs. About the team and the career he loved. He couldn't do it alone, that was for sure.

Help me do the right thing, whatever that might be. To sacrifice for her if that's what it takes to be sure she's safe.

He opened the door, and they stopped in front of the colonel's middle-aged assistant's desk. She plumped her chin-length black hair, but it looked stiff from hair spray and didn't move.

"Is the colonel in?" Claire asked.

She nodded and smiled at them.

"I need to see him." Claire put a sense of urgency into her tone that would be hard to refuse. "It's about the urgent matter he has me working on."

The assistant picked up her phone and held a short, but convincing conversation. "You can go in."

Travis let Claire enter first and then followed her into the large office that was as neat and tidy as would be expected of a colonel. He displayed awards, mementos, and photos on a wall-to-wall bookshelf behind his desk and on the other walls.

The bald man, about six two, stood and pressed out a crease in his uniform. "Dr. Reed. Chapman. Have a seat."

"Thank you, sir." Claire dropped into a hard wooden chair as if plopping on a plush sofa. Maybe her legs were weak with stress from Travis mentioning that she might have a stalker for life. She needed to know, but he should've kept his big mouth shut until this was all over.

"How can I help?" Lynch sat.

Claire brought him up to speed on Robb. "We think it was just an attempt to stalk me, but he did film videos which would've made him privy to private work information."

"I'm sorry you had to put up with a stalker, Claire." Lynch clenched his jaw, and Travis suspected the guy wanted to give Robb a talking to as well.

"I made it clear that if he ever saw the light of day again, he better not come anywhere close to her," Travis said.

"Glad to hear that." Lynch firmed his shoulders. "We'll throw the book at him. We can't condone theft of our information no matter the thief's intention. And well, if you ask me, a man who stalks a woman shouldn't be allowed to live among us."

Claire grimaced. "I thought you might say that."

"Looks like you don't agree with my decision," Lynch said.

Claire didn't answer right away but stared out the side window. "I don't know how I feel, sir. It's all too much right now."

"Then let me relieve some of your stress by handling the arrest for you. I know a local police captain, and I'll get on the horn to him. We'll get Robb picked up and processed right away."

"Thank you." Claire let out a long breath and gave him what looked like a forced smile.

"Any luck in finding our actual thief?" Lynch asked.

Travis explained what was happening at the motel right now. "We'll let you know the moment we have concrete proof of White's action."

"White." Lynch shook his head. "Never would've pegged him for a traitor. We have any motives for his theft?"

"No," Travis said. "Our investigation hasn't turned anything up."

"Probably money or revenge," Lynch said. "At least that's what most traitors are after."

Claire clasped the arms of her chair. "I don't think Warren was ever wronged, but you never know. I didn't think Mike was a stalker either."

"Hopefully he'll enlighten us when he's arrested." Lynch stood and planted his hands on the desktop. "Good job. Both of you. Now if you'll excuse me, I'll make that call to have Robb arrested."

Claire and Travis turned to leave.

"Any decision on the job offer yet, Chapman?" Lynch asked.

Claire flashed her shocked gaze to Travis. "Job offer?"

Travis had to ignore Claire right now. Lynch knew nothing about their former relationship and would wonder why Claire was upset. Not Travis. He didn't wonder at all. He'd kept this big news from her and hurt her in the process. He should've figured it would get back to her and told her right up front. Man, he screwed up big time.

But right now, he had to get them out of this office. He glanced back at the colonel. "Nothing yet, sir. I'll get back to you the minute I decide."

Claire exited Lynch's office and raced past his assistant. Travis kept up and pulled the door closed behind him as he knew an explosion was coming.

Claire spun in the hallway to lock a disappointed gaze on him. "He offered you a job here? Here at my institute? And you didn't think to mention it?"

What did he say that wouldn't make her even more disappointed in him for withholding vital information? The truth. That was all he had on his side. "I thought it best to keep it to myself until I had time to think about it."

"I wish you would've trusted me with it." She blinked a few times and marched away.

He'd screwed up. She still had feelings for him. Just like he had feelings for her. And not consulting her on the offer had hurt her big time. He'd thought he'd done the right thing, trying not to cause her any pain if he decided not to take the job.

In the end, he'd hurt her all the more, and he didn't know if they could come back from his dumb mistake.

17

Eryn had come through for them again. Travis couldn't be more thankful for her skills because this was all over now. Almost anyway. They still had to take White down. Travis should trust the police to nab the thief, but he didn't. Nor did his team. Or maybe he just wanted to be the one to look the man in the eye and tell him they knew what he'd done. Then recover the prototype and give it back to Claire. To set her free from her worry.

Maybe a peace offering for his screw-up. Yeah, that too, because she hadn't talked to him—looked at him—since they'd left Lynch's office.

"I'm coming with you," she stated but stared over his shoulder.

"This isn't up for discussion," Travis said.

She flashed her disappointed gaze up to him. "You mean like the job offer?"

"This is nothing like a job offer," he said, wishing she hadn't brought it up. "This is dangerous."

She tilted her head and studied him. He felt like one of many palmetto bugs, a fancy name for a cockroach around here, that she would lift her foot over to squash.

"I'll wait in the SUV," she said. "But once you have Warren, I want to talk to him."

"Things could go south. I can't risk it."

"With four spec ops guys and a former FBI agent against a network security manager?" She cocked a brow. "Not likely."

"Things happen."

"You're overreacting," she said. "I'll be going with or without you. I think it's better if I'm with you, right?"

"Fine. You win." He tried to contain his frustration but he didn't manage it at all. "But I'll sit out the takedown and wait in the car with you."

"No need."

"I think there is." He held out his hand. "The others are waiting. Let's go."

He followed her to the exit. With Robb behind bars and Gage having eyes on White, she wasn't in danger. He whipped open the door and then marched her out to the vehicle driven by Coop.

Claire slid in the back behind Jackson, who rode shotgun.

Both men raised their eyebrows at that, but Travis shook his head to warn them off questioning. "Let's move."

They rode in silence to the motel, where they parked on the far side of the lot by Gage's vehicle. He was leaning against the front of the SUV with Eryn standing next to him. The building was a long, two-story, run-down affair with faded blue paint and a blinking neon sign at the road. Just the kind of place where a guy up to no good went to hide out.

Travis looked at Claire. "Stay here while I update Gage on the plan."

He slid out and got the SUV keys from Coop before he joined his buddy.

Gage eyed him. "You brought Claire?"

"It was either that, or she would've driven herself." Travis tried to keep his anger in check. "I'll remain in the vehicle with her while you all take White down. Text me when it's safe for her to enter his room so she can talk to him."

"You know I don't like that," Gage said. "Things happen."

"I don't either, but we don't have a choice if we don't want her to interfere in the takedown."

Gage handed a comms unit to Travis. "You can listen in, and you'll be able to see us breach the room from here. I'll let you know when we're ready for her."

"Let's do this by the book," Travis said. "We don't want this guy skating."

Gage nodded. "I've scouted the place. No windows in the room except the front one. Eryn, you'll knock. Pretend to be looking for someone else. We'll hang to the side out of his view. The minute that door opens, you push your way in. We'll be right behind you, weapons drawn. Since you can't have your weapon out without alerting him, fade to the left, and we'll take him down."

"Roger that." Her excitement for the op shone in her eyes.

Travis's frustration over missing the takedown grew.

Eryn glanced at her teammates. "We'll see if you bad boys can keep up with my fade."

They chuckled, and Travis liked Eryn even more. She was the complete package. Smart. Skilled in IT. And possessed tactical skills too. Just the kind of person Gage would have on his team.

"Okay, any questions?" Gage asked.

"Usual stack order?" Coop asked.

Gage nodded.

Travis didn't bother asking the order that they lined up

in when preparing to breach a door. Stack order didn't matter to him, but it did for them. A consistent stack told each operator what to expect of the guy in front of and behind him. And Travis suspected their stack had to do with their injuries and how each man made up for the other one in the event that their bodies failed.

"Any other questions?" Gage asked.

"Nah," Jackson said. "It's a pretty straightforward and simple op."

"Still," Gage said. "Don't let that make you complacent and let your guard down. That's when bad things happen."

"Roger that," Jackson said.

Gage signaled for his team to move out, and the warriors marched off, heading straight for the motel.

Travis went back to the vehicle and slid behind the wheel. He considered inviting Claire up front, but she was better off in the second row where she could hit the floor if needed. He fired up the engine in the event that he had to make a quick exit. He locked the doors and focused on the motel room.

"I'm sorry you're missing out," she said. "It wasn't my intent. You've worked hard to resolve this. In fact, without you and your resources, we still wouldn't know who stole the prototype."

"No worries," he said and tried to sound convincing. He tapped his earbud. "Now I need to listen into the op in case it goes south, and we need to evacuate."

"Oh, sure. Right."

Great. She sounded hurt again. He wanted to fix things, but he couldn't now. Not when his attention was needed on the takedown.

He watched and listened in, his pulse kicking up. The team made their way to the motel, where they moved parallel to the building, a tactical move to keep White from making them.

Near the door, Gage stopped and held up his hand. "You're on, Eryn. Be your most convincing and get this guy to open his door."

Eryn released her hair from a rubber band holding it back then shook it out. It fell in sleek black waves over her shoulders. Not many men would likely resist opening the door to her, but then White was hiding out and could be highly unpredictable.

She knocked on the door. "Becky. It's me. Eryn. Open up."

She stood back a bit so White could get a clear view of her in the peephole.

Travis counted down. One. Two. Three. Hit twenty-five and the door came open.

Eryn didn't speak but shoved hard, pushing White back. Coop barreled inside. Then Jackson. Gage last.

"Hands. Hands. Hands where we can see them," the men called out.

"Got him," Coop's voice rose above the others.

"What's going on?" Had to be White speaking. "You must've mistaken me for someone else."

"Are you Warren White?" Gage asked.

"Yes."

"Then no mistake," Gage said. "We're here to detain you until the police arrive to arrest you for theft."

"Theft? Theft of what?" White challenged.

"Of that prototype sitting on the dresser," Gage said.

"Looks like they found the prototype," Travis told Claire. "Not one hundred percent sure, but sounds like it."

"Praise God!" She slumped in the seat. "This is over then. Truly over."

Gage's voice came over Travis's earbud. "We're clear for Claire."

"Do you still feel a need to confront White?" Travis asked her.

"I do."

"Then let's go." He killed the engine and slid out into the heat. She joined him.

"Stay close to me," he said. "Just in case."

"Can do."

They made a direct trip across the lot to the room. White was seated on the bed, his hands behind him, most likely zip-tied. He flashed his gaze to Claire. "You have to tell them this is a mistake."

Gage pointed at the prototype sitting on a long, scarred dresser.

"Then explain why you have the prototype," she said, looking like she was working hard to control herself from saying so much more.

White lifted his chin and looked her in the eye. "I heard it was stolen and got it back."

Travis snorted.

"Let's try that answer again." Eryn explained how she tracked his transmission for the theft to the motel.

"I was just testing our security," he said, still peering at Claire. "You have to believe me."

Claire let out a long breath. "If that was true, why not loop me in on the test?"

"I...I...well, I didn't want it getting out."

"Who did you recover the prototype from?" Travis asked.

"I...I mean, some guy I tracked down."

"How?" Claire demanded. "You know the security feed was cut. There was no footage so how did you find someone all of these fine investigators and a top-notch forensics lab couldn't locate?"

He swallowed hard. "My mistake. I must be thinking of something else. I don't remember now."

Claire's eyes darkened and she stepped closer to glare down on White. "How could you betray us like this? We worked together for six years. Day in and day out. I thought you cared almost as much as I did about this project."

His chin went up higher. "Did you ever think we aren't all like you and some of us wanted to have a life outside of the job?"

Claire narrowed her eyes. "You didn't have to put in so many hours."

"If I wanted to keep my job, I did."

"I never told you that."

"Unspoken."

"You could've left. Found another job." She eyed him, "Oh, wait. You didn't want to risk it, did you? Risk the world finding out you're really Fitz Ellwood."

He sucked in a breath. "I don't know what you're talking about."

"Yes, you do," she said. "And we can prove it."

"Good luck with that," he mumbled.

She lifted her shoulders. "You still have living family, and DNA is powerful proof of identity."

"We have the top forensic team in the country on our side," Travis said. "They'll investigate the murder of Ross Garland, and you'll go away for that too."

White's already pale skin lost all color.

"I'm done here," Claire said. "Let's bring in the police and have this loser hauled in."

White sneered at her. "You always thought you were so special. Better than all of us. Well, you're not. You're just a workaholic with zero life of your own, so you have to ruin ours. Thankfully, I'm done with that."

"Yeah." She spun. "Enjoy the rest of your life behind

bars. Between espionage and murder charges, you'll never be free again."

She marched out the door and got out her phone. Her breathing was deep and rapid, her eyes glistening with tears.

As Travis had thought, it hadn't been a good idea to confront White. His last comment was way too harsh. Though Travis had to admit there was a hint of truth about Claire being a workaholic. But she didn't ruin other people's lives. White had a choice to work the hours he did. Claire would never expect him to give up everything—as she'd done.

"Colonel Lynch. Good. I'm glad I caught you. Warren White has been detained, and he was in possession of the prototype." She gave him the details, her words tumbling out in a rush. She didn't mention White's final comment, but listened intently and then ended her call.

She looked at Travis and shoved her phone back into her pocket. "Lynch is calling in the police, but I can't stay here. You were right. I shouldn't have come. I don't feel better."

"You didn't ruin his life, Claire," he said. "We have free will to do what we choose, and he could've shortened his hours or like you told him, found a different job."

"But I am a workaholic."

"Yes," he said honestly. "Doesn't mean you expect the same from those who work for you."

She let out a slow breath. "Do you mind driving me back to work? I want to tell Julie what happened and why I've been so off with her this week. Then I want to go home. Alone."

He watched her for a long moment. She looked like she might cave.

"Please," she added.

He got it. Loud and clear. She didn't want him in her life. "Let me tell Gage we're leaving, and then we can go."

She gave a halfhearted nod.

He poked his head in the door to inform Gage of their decision and then it hit him.

This was over.

Claire's stalker was in police custody and soon White would be as well. She was no longer in danger. The stolen software and hardware were recovered. She didn't need him and would send him packing again. Unless he did something about it. Not something. Unless he left the team.

Something he still had no idea if he was capable of doing.

~

It was over. Really over and Claire was free to resume her life tonight. Good, right? Then why did she feel so empty? Alone. Sitting around in her house thinking didn't help. She grabbed her vacuum and ran it over the floor to keep herself occupied. She didn't want to think about how she ended things with Travis.

"Face it," she mumbled. "You also don't like that Travis isn't here."

I really, really don't want to be alone. Reality hit hard and her feet stilled.

She'd loved being with Travis. Both in the past and since he'd returned to Orlando. Loved every minute of it, even the tense, raw moments. The way he made her feel proved she was alive. Fully alive. Not the shell of a woman she'd been since her dad's death. She'd simply been going through the motions of life, but not really living. Except when she was with Travis. He brought out her desire to live life to the fullest. Something well worth the risk of losing him to some unknown foe.

Convinced to tell him how she felt as soon as she saw him again, she continued across the room with a lighter step. Her phone flashed on the table. A text from Julie.

You won't believe what I discovered about the theft. Can you come to the office so I can show something to you?

Yes, she replied without giving it more consideration. She could only vacuum so long and she still wanted to get away from her own thoughts. But Travis should know there was some news on the theft. She started to call him.

Her doorbell rang. Could it be Travis?

She rushed to the door and looked out the peephole. Her heart fell.

Only Detective Purcell.

She pulled the door open. "Detective. How can I help you?"

"I was hoping to get an official statement from you regarding Warren White." He smiled.

"I'm just on my way out." She explained about the new lead.

"Sounds like it relates to the theft, and I should come with you."

She would rather go alone, but if she argued, he would insist.

"You're welcome to come along. Let me make a quick call, and then I'm ready to go." She dialed Travis and got his voicemail. She told him where she was going with Purcell and to join her if he got the message in time.

She dropped her phone into her purse and got out her keys. "I'll drive. The security booth is unmanned on weekend nights, and the barcode that opens the gate is mounted on my dash."

"I...well...okay." He looked uncomfortable with leaving

his vehicle behind, but he radioed in their plan and then joined her in her car.

Excitement over the lead had her chatting nervously about the weather as she drove, and she nearly missed her first turn. She hooked a quick right, and Purcell eyed her, but she ignored him and placed her focus squarely on the road.

A car suddenly pulled from the curb in front of her, forcing her to hit the brakes.

"That guy would get a ticket if I was in my vehicle," Purcell mumbled.

The car slowed more and a large SUV pulled out behind them and raced toward her bumper.

Purcell swiveled to look behind them. His expression shifted from surprise to grim understanding. "It's a trap. They're gonna squeeze us until we're forced to stop." He drew his gun. "Try to go around the car."

Her hands shook, but she held it together to swerve to the side. Both cars reacted quickly, keeping her sandwiched between them. The SUV's powerful engine roared, and the vehicle slammed into her bumper.

The car in front jerked to a stop, and she stomped on the brakes. The tires screeched and the car skidded. Slid sideways. Barreling closer to the car in front.

She pumped harder on the brakes. They couldn't stop. She braced herself. Her vehicle slammed into the car. The crash deafening. Her airbag deployed, slapping her in the face and knocking the breath out of her. Purcell's bag inflated too. She fought with hers, punching the fabric to try to deflate it. He shoved his out of his way.

"Stay here." He eased out of the car. Staying low, he slid along the side of her vehicle, heading for the rear.

A gunshot rang out.

What in the world?

She was a sitting duck. Panic hit her. She fumbled to release her seat belt and dived for the passenger's seat to glance out the open door at Purcell. He'd dropped to the ground, his hand pressed on something.

"Are you okay?" she screamed.

He didn't move. Reply.

No. No. No. Was he hit?

She had to check on him. She slipped out. Caught sight of a man bolting from the front vehicle.

The shooter? Was he coming to kill her too? She was defenseless.

Purcell's gun. She had to get to Purcell's gun.

She scrambled toward him. Moved inch after inch. Footfalls crunching her way, sounding in her head like giant rolls of thunder from one of the many Orlando thunderstorms. She made it three feet. Hands jerked her back by the shoulders. An arm clamped around her waist and lifted her.

She bucked and kicked, twisting with all her might.

"Give it a rest, Claire," a familiar voice sounded in her ear. "Don't scream or the chloroform comes out again. Got it?"

"Eric?" His name eased past the lump in her throat.

"Surprise." He lifted her up and walked to his car. All those years of bodybuilding allowed him to carry her as if she were a small child.

Julie's Eric. Really? He was involved in the theft? Was Julie implicated in this too? Was that why she'd sent the text tonight?

The sting of betrayal bit hard, cutting Claire to the core. Eric opened his trunk and dropped her inside. Gone were the thoughts of betrayal. Now it was all about survival. Should she scream? No point on this deserted stretch of road. Maybe she could get away once he closed the trunk.

He grabbed her hands. Forced them behind her back

and secured them with a rough rope. He moved to her ankles. He was taking no chances. He grabbed a rag. Shoved it into her mouth. She gagged. Fought to breathe.

He scowled at her. "You could've just given me the code, and it wouldn't have to come to this."

She wanted to spout back at him. He'd made sure she couldn't. Not respond to his comment or say anything to anyone.

He slammed the trunk with a resounding thud.

Darkness settled in. Cloying. Fearful. Black.

No. No. No. She had to get out of there. She just had to.

The car's engine roared to life.

Her heart raced. *Thump. Thump. Thump.* Pounding as if it could help her get out of this predicament. She struggled against the ropes. The rough fibers tore at her skin, but didn't budge.

Panic blanketed her, cutting off her air.

Stop. Save your strength.

Yes, she had to rest. She would need every ounce of energy if she wanted to get out of this alive.

18

Disgusted, Travis cranked the engine on his car. He didn't like that they hadn't resolved Kent's lie of working nights, and he didn't want Claire to be working with a man who lied without knowing what he was hiding. So Travis had staked the guy out and tailed him to the house of a woman who worked at the institute. She met him at the door. Their kiss and embrace made the reason for his visit clear. He was having an affair. Most likely explained his whereabouts at night and the lies to his wife.

His behavior made Travis sick. If he was ever lucky enough to have a wife—lucky enough to have someone like Claire—he'd never sully his vows that way.

Claire. Maybe she'd been the one who called him while he was driving to the woman's house.

He dug his phone out and saw a missed call and voice-mail from her. He played the message. She'd gone to work to meet Julie about the theft. What in the world had Julie discovered?

He needed to know. He shifted into gear and pointed his SUV for the institute, the roads deserted and dark. He neared the building, and his phone rang. Caller ID declared the institute.

"Claire," he answered.

"No, it's Julie." Her panicked tone hit Travis like a physical punch to the gut. "Claire's been in a car accident."

His heart plummeted. "Is she okay?"

"I don't know. We don't know where she is."

"Then how in thunder do you know she's been in an accident?" He'd snapped and instantly regretted it.

"She's testing a new phone app we're developing for military vehicles. If she's in an accident and her phone's mounted on her dash, the app senses the collision and starts the video recording on her phone. Then it sends an email to Peter Fisk, who's the project supervisor. He's downloading the data now. We'll know more soon."

"I'm right outside. Meet me at the gate to let me in." He cranked the wheel hard and jerked to a stop until the gate lifted. Within minutes, they were in Peter's office with introductions out of the way.

"I've already had a chance to review the video, but honestly, it's too dark to get any idea of where the accident occurred." Peter ran a hand over his head. "I've already used her phone's GPS to try to locate her, but she doesn't have it turned on."

"She didn't like to leave her GPS turned on," Julie said. "Except for apps that need it when she's using them."

Feeling helpless, Travis peered at Peter. "Can you track the email and get a location of where it originated?"

"Not without the help of her cell phone service provider." Peter held up a hand. "Before you get excited about that, even if I could find someone to talk to me at the phone company, they won't share private information with me. It would take police involvement to get a warrant for it, and that could take time."

Time they didn't have. "Then let's look at the video to see if we can figure out her location."

Peter started the video playing and tapped the screen. "That jarring of the camera you see is the point of impact. Since Claire was hit from behind, her front-facing camera caught this video of the back of her car."

The camera settled, displaying a large SUV forcing her car forward then the screen suddenly changed. Travis wished for sound to hear Claire's voice, but they only had video.

"Now she slams into the car in front of her," Peter said. "And the phone changes to the rear-facing camera, catching everything in front of her car, including the guy who's with her."

"Detective Purcell," Travis said.

A smaller sedan came to a complete stop, which in turn jerked Claire's car to a stop. The sedan inched several feet ahead, but Claire's vehicle didn't move.

"So it's a minor fender bender," Travis said, his senses still on high alert. "I don't understand why she didn't call me."

"Keep watching," Peter said.

The driver's door on the sedan opened, and a man climbed out. He raised a gun and rested his arm on the roof, his face shadowed in the darkness of night. The muzzle flashed, and the man's arm jerked.

Travis's heart stopped. He could almost hear the gunshot reverberate through the night. Feel the recoil of the weapon. See the target fall.

"Did he just shoot someone?" Julie's voice skyrocketed high.

"Looks like it," Travis said, but kept his eyes glued to the screen, dreading confirmation that the gunman had shot Claire. Was it wrong to hope he'd shot Purcell instead?

Weapon pointed ahead, he marched toward her car. He crossed between the vehicles and disappeared from the video. When he returned on screen, he had Claire clamped in his arms. She was kicking and thrashing, but he managed to get the trunk open and drop her inside.

"She's alive," Julie said on a whispered breath.

A weight was lifted from Travis's shoulders. Momentary. He couldn't relax. Claire was still in extreme danger. He kept his eyes riveted to the screen. To Claire. Headlights from her car caught the terror in her eyes, making Travis furious and light-headed at the same time.

He waited for Purcell to come to Claire's rescue, but there was no sign of the detective. Which meant he'd been incapacitated. Likely was the one who'd been shot.

Travis flashed a quick look at Peter. "Would you call 911 to report the shooting?"

"I did the moment I saw the video. They're already looking for Detective Purcell."

Travis prayed the police had some way of tracking their detective. Maybe finding Claire too, but it looked as if her abductor planned to take her from the scene.

He retrieved a rope then wound it around her wrists and ankles, drawing it tight. He shoved a rag in her mouth. Travis curled his hands into fists. He would pummel this guy the second he found him.

He closed the trunk then turned, the headlights clearly illuminating his face.

Julie gasped and dropped into a chair.

"Eric?" Travis spun on her. "Did you know about this?"

"The abduction? No."

"But you had something to do with the theft."

She cringed but said nothing.

Travis advanced on her, giving her a look guaranteed to break even the most reluctant subject in one of his interrogations. "If you know what's good for you, you'll tell me everything."

"I stole the prototype," she admitted, shrinking back in her chair. "But not to sell it—honest!"

He bought her answer, but should he? "Then why?"

"I'm tired of living in Claire's shadow, okay." She sat up, her shoulders and chin lifted. "Always being second in charge when I'm just as qualified. I wanted to take Claire down a peg. Let the people in charge of the institute look to me for once. When Eric suggested stealing the prototype to make her look bad, I went for it."

Travis gaped at her. "And you let your boyfriend attack her?"

She shot up a hand. "No...no...wait. I didn't know he was behind the attacks. You have to believe me. I honestly thought someone was stalking her." She wrung her hands. "I even talked to Eric, and he promised he wasn't the one responsible."

"And just like that you believed him?"

"Claire said you had no proof of who attacked her, so I thought you'd made a mistake by thinking it was related to the prototype theft."

"Good point, but with two cars involved in this abduction, he's obviously working with someone."

"I didn't know that."

Travis took a breath to clear his brain and process before moving on. "How does Warren White fit in with this?"

"Warren?" Julie scrunched her eyes. "He's not involved."

"He is."

She blinked rapidly. "Are you sure?"

"We caught him today with the prototype and software on his laptop." Travis held her gaze. "He's already behind bars."

"No wonder," she whispered.

"No wonder what?" Travis asked.

She clutched her hands together and cowered in her chair.

Travis moved closer to her. "Tell me, Julie. Claire's life could depend on it."

"Tonight," she said. "Eric asked to meet me here. So I did. Then he said wouldn't it be great if we took the other prototype too. To bring the program to a complete stop. Then they would have to fire Claire, and I would get the job."

"So you let him take it?" Travis had to work hard not to shout at her.

She nodded. "I don't know why he gave the other one to Warren, but maybe Warren was in on this the whole time. He and Eric met at a work party and have gone out for drinks a few times to compare work notes."

"Seems like Eric kept a lot from you."

"Yeah. Yeah, it does." She frowned.

"You didn't send the text to get Claire over here, did you?" Travis asked as his thoughts cleared, and he started to process his next steps.

"I didn't text her." Julie dug out her phone and stared at the screen, tears forming in her eyes. "I can't believe it. Eric must've sent the text when I was in the bathroom."

She paused for a moment and lifted her eyes to the ceiling. "Maybe I should've seen the signs. He's having financial issues. He comes from a very wealthy family and is used to having the finest things in life. He's well paid, but he spends it all and more. His parents could help him, but they refuse." She wrapped her arms around her waist. "I didn't know he was this desperate. I just didn't know."

Travis didn't want to believe her, but she seemed to be telling the truth. He'd met Eric and hadn't suspected the guy, so why wouldn't a woman blinded by love fail to notice his duplicitous behavior? Either way it didn't matter.

Eric had Claire, and Travis needed to find her. "He would take her someplace private. Anywhere come to mind?"

Julie tapped a finger on her chin as precious seconds ticked by.

"Think!" Travis shouted, making her jump. "Where would he take her?"

"His family has a private compound on the outskirts of Orlando."

"Tell me about it."

"They have several thousand acres with a few cabins near a lake. His parents have their own plane so there's an airstrip. The rest of the land is swampy."

The perfect place to hide someone—and maybe even dispose of someone. *"Tell me how to get there."*

She rattled off directions. "It's very remote with only a narrow lane leading to the cabins. If he's there he'll see you arrive."

"Which might make him panic." Travis ran over the scenarios he might employ for a rescue. "You said there's an airstrip. How close is it to the cabin?"

"Maybe a half mile."

"Far enough away for someone to parachute in without being seen?"

"I guess so."

Travis dug out his phone to call his CO and arrange for a helicopter to the compound.

Let me be doing the right thing here. And keep Claire safe until I can get to her.

~

Eric freed Claire's ankles, and she wanted to rub away the rough patches from the scratchy rope, but he left her wrists bound.

He pulled the rag from her mouth. She coughed and tried to swallow, but her mouth was desert dry.

"Don't bother shouting for help or screaming." He smirked. "My parents own several thousand acres around here, and no one will hear you."

Several thousand acres. Where in the world were they, and how was anyone going to find her?

He jerked her out and set her on her feet.

She tried to get moisture back into her mouth. She could barely swallow, but she forgot about it for a moment to take in her surroundings. The long driveway led up to tall tropical plants surrounding a cabin. More like a large house with a cabin design.

The other direction led to a swampy area that had raised walkways heading somewhere she couldn't determine in the darkness of night.

He jerked her forward, dragging her up the stairs, where he tapped a code into the keyless entry pad. He flipped on lights to a large vaulted family room with a big dining room and kitchen abutting the open space.

He shoved her into a chair at the dining table. "I'll get you some water."

She thought to run, but she knew she couldn't outrun him, and she needed to keep hydrated for when the opportunity presented itself for her to take off.

He retrieved two expensive-looking bottles of water from a commercial-size stainless steel refrigerator. "If you promise not to try anything, I'll untie your hands."

She wouldn't promise any such thing and mean it. "Okay."

He freed the rope, and it fell to the floor.

She brought her arms around, the muscles screaming in agony.

He gave her the water.

"Why are you doing this?" she asked.

"I suppose you deserve to know." He cracked his water bottle open as if they were hanging out at a coffee shop instead of him abducting her. "I lost money in an investment and needed a quick infusion of cash. So I borrowed it from a loan shark. Figured I had enough time to pay it back. Didn't work out that way so this was the best solution."

Big long shot as far as she could see. "How did you get into the building to steal the prototype?"

"I didn't. Julie did."

Claire sat forward. "She what?"

"Newsflash. She doesn't like taking second place to you all the time. She's qualified to do your job, and you're taking all the glory when she does all the grunt work."

"I do my share of grunt work. A lot of things she never even sees. Besides, she never said anything."

"She shouldn't have to. She's your friend. You should've seen it."

He was right. If Julie was unhappy, Claire should've picked up on it. "I'm sorry if that happened."

"Well, it did." He shrugged as if he didn't care. "But it helped me until you refused to give up the code, and the loan shark learned the device had no value without that. He demanded I figure it out or we would have to get it out of you."

"That explains some things, but I don't get when and why Warren got involved?"

"He was in it from the beginning. I offered him a cut if he helped us steal the software and then figure out the missing piece. But he screwed up somehow and got busted. Lost the prototype."

"Why would he help you?"

"Simple." A cocky smile crossed his face. "I blackmailed him."

"With what?"

"One night he got drunk and told me he killed a guy in a boating accident and assumed this guy's identity. He was putty in my hands after that."

"He couldn't have helped you tonight, so who did?"

"Loan shark's been most helpful all along. His guy was the one who tried to haul you into the van."

"Explains why your face isn't bruised."

"Couldn't damage this pretty face." He cackled. "My guy also gave me the chloroform and sent a guy to drive the vehicle that rear-ended you."

"And now?"

"Now." He shrugged. "If you don't give me the specs tonight, I'll kill Travis."

She gasped.

"Yeah. Thought you'd react that way."

"What makes you think you can kill someone as skilled as Travis?"

He went to a gun cabinet in the family room and pulled out a rifle. He aimed it at her and a red laser dot landed on her hand before slithering up her body. "I've won every sharpshooting contest I could enter. He doesn't expect me, so I could take him out from such a long distance he wouldn't even know I was there."

She wanted to gasp again but stifled it. She couldn't let the man she loved die. Maybe if she told Eric what he wanted she could buy time to get away.

"Give me paper and a pen, and I'll write down the code."

He produced a notepad and pen and looked down on her, a maniacal grin spreading over his mouth.

Chills ran down her, but she started writing. Slowly as he watched. She paused at intervals to stretch her back and pretend to rub raw wrists that she wouldn't even want to touch.

He got out his phone. Walked into the kitchen. Informed whoever was on the other end that he had the code. The loan shark? Likely.

He lowered his voice. Started talking about how to get rid of her once she was done giving them the code.

She couldn't just sit there. She bolted for the door.

Wrenched it open.

Eric's footfalls followed. She glanced back and saw him snatch up the rifle. She picked up speed, racing down the steps toward the swamp.

His footsteps charged after her.

He could shoot her in the back. So what? He was going to kill her anyway, and at least she hadn't given him the code before she died.

The helicopter rotors thumped through the night, whirring Travis closer to the compound.

"Going black." The pilot's words carried over Travis's headset.

The chopper went dark except for the faint glow from the instrument panels.

His heart racing, Travis signaled for his pilot to bank right and drop him nearby. He would've liked to fast-rope down instead of free-falling, but the sound of a helo hovering close to the ground would alert Eric.

He checked his gear a final time.

The door opened.

He caught a glimpse through his goggles of Claire

bolting from the cabin. Racing across the lawn. Heading straight for alligator-infested swamps.

No!

A man darted outside behind her. A rifle to his shoulder, he moved at a rapid clip. Faster. Faster. Hot on her tail.

Travis squinted. Zoomed in on his face.

Eric.

She'd escaped. Was running from him. Good? Maybe not. Was it better to be free if she was charging into alligator country?

Travis burned to help. But how? With his rifle strapped to his back, he could do nothing to help her from his altitude. Nothing.

He had to get down there. Now. Quickly.

Don't overreact. Follow your plan.

Even if, after seeing her, he'd like to call an audible and land closer. He couldn't. Not without risking a bullet to the gut during his descent.

He signaled for his pilot to bank right and drop him nearby.

The chopper tipped. He looked out the opposite window. Good. The police and an ambulance waited out of sight for his signal. His backup. Green Berets might often be accused of trying to be heroes, but Claire was too important for him to go solo.

But could he get to her in time? Could he?

Panic swallowed him whole. Panic he'd never known as an operator.

Calm down. She needs you at your best not as a basket case.

"Approaching target." The pilot's deep voice startled Travis.

Go time.

He signaled his readiness and dropped into the night sky. Black with stars glittering overhead. Gravity pulled him downward. Down. Down. Down. The wind rushed up to meet him, catching his chute and jerking him upright. He directed the fabric toward his landing target.

His heart thumped in his chest, the pounding like a conga drum in his head.

Keep it together, man. You'll get to her in time. Eric needs her alive.

Or does he? She might've already provided Eric with the specs.

Now his goal was to silence her.

Forever.

And Travis was powerless to stop him.

19

———

Claire pounded over the spongy ground, her every sense attuned to the night hanging thick and heavy overhead. To the slight breeze carrying fetid smells from the swamp. The insects buzzing. The darkness suffocating and paralyzing as she raced through it. No matter her fear, she had to keep going.

Her life depended on it.

Eric was gaining on her now, his footfalls pounding closer.

Fear raised its ugly head. *Faster. Go faster.*

She tried to pick up speed. Swampy gunk sucked at her feet and threatened to take her down. Slowing her more. Her only hope was to hide. But where?

Think, Claire, think.

She slowed and searched the area. A pool of stagnant water lay ahead. As a native Floridian, Eric had to know water meant gators. If she took to the water, he would never follow. She didn't have the same choice. She would rather chance making it safely to the other side before Eric spotted her than stay on shore and risk a certain bullet to the back.

Holding her hands high to keep the slimy water from

the raw circles the rope left on her wrists, she plunged in. Cool water swallowed her ankles. Thankfully, her ankles hadn't suffered the same injury or the pain might slow her down even more.

She moved at a snail's pace. The bottom, slimy sludge, slowing her down.

Five feet.

Ten. Twenty. Thirty. Movement rippled the water at her side.

A gator? Probably.

Terrified, she dug deeper. Picked up speed, churning the foul water. A dark form emerged about ten feet away.

No, oh, no. It really is a gator.

A big one. Silent. Deadly. Gliding toward her. Water sluicing off his rough hide. His beady eyes skimming over the surface and fixed on her. His jaw poised and ready to snap.

Oh, God, please don't let me die this way or even be injured. Please!

She dug her shoes in and pushed with all her might. The quicksand of a bottom captured her feet. The water shifted more.

Now only three feet away.

Please, not this!

A crack split the night, and the gator stilled. She spun. Saw a man wearing goggles on the bank with a rifle to his shoulder.

Eric? Or maybe his associate?

She was safe from the gator now, but she hadn't made it safely to the other side where she could hide. If it *was* Eric, he must see her. So why would he kill the gator when he could've put the same bullet in her back?

"Claire," the man called out as he lowered the weapon.

His voice wrapped around her like a blanket. "Travis. Is that you?"

"It's me."

"You found me." She started sobbing. "You really found me."

"Shh, honey. You don't want to attract any more of those shoes in the making, do you?" He laughed, and it rumbled through the mist helping her gain control of her tears. "I'll keep an eye out for another one while you hightail it over here."

"Be careful," she warned as she slipped toward shore. "Eric's after me, and he has a gun."

"Not anymore."

She heard the certainty in his voice. He'd subdued her foe. Both man and beast.

She couldn't believe this wonderful, amazing man was in her life. The man who readily gave of himself so others might be safe. Gave of himself so *she* might be safe. The man she loved and wanted to spend the rest of her life with, if he'd have her.

And she planned to tell him that as soon as she escaped the swamp without becoming a gator snack.

Claire's plan to declare her love had been a good one. Too bad she couldn't pull it off. Not with police sirens cutting into the night and a very demanding police officer stepping between her and Travis.

In the glow from the headlights of the officer's car, Travis gave the short, stocky officer a rundown of the events and offered the location where he'd bound Eric to a tree.

The officer clamped a hand on his sidearm. "We'll take him into custody right away."

"Promise me you'll secure the stolen prototype and specs too," Claire said. "I don't want to risk Eric getting free and taking it from the house."

The officer nodded and glanced between them. "We need statements from you both and will separate you until we can get them."

"No." Travis fired a sharp look at the officer that would make Claire run for the hills.

The officer didn't even flinch but widened his stance. "It's protocol."

"I don't care about protocol." Travis raised his voice and folded his arms across his broad chest. "I'm not leaving this woman's side ever again."

Detective Purcell, his arm in a sling, joined them. His gaze shot between Travis and the officer, then settled on Travis. "We can let protocol slide this time if you and Dr. Reed agree not to discuss the incident before we take your statements."

"You have my word," Travis responded quickly.

"Then after the medic clears Dr. Reed for travel, I'll give you both a lift to the station, and we'll get those official statements." Purcell focused on the cop. "Let's give them some time alone."

"Wait, your arm," Claire said. "You're really okay to be here?"

Purcell lifted his arm. "Just a scratch."

She studied his face, pain written in his expression. "But you were unconscious."

"Hit my head when I went down. Was only out for a few minutes, and I'm good to go now." He jerked his head, signaling for the officer to join him.

The officer's expression tightened, but he followed Purcell as they headed for the tree where Travis said they would find Eric.

Claire let out a long breath, the tension of the night flowing with it. "He's lying of course. He's not fine. Exactly what you would do to complete a mission."

"Yeah, but if he really wasn't good to be up and about, he would've been kept at the ER."

She scooted closer to Travis. Even in the haziness, she tried to telegraph her feelings for him in a single look. "I hoped you would come."

"Did you now?"

She nodded. "Next time, don't wait so long, okay?"

With a laugh, he swooped her into his arms and crushed her to his chest. If only the police would finish setting up their portable lights, she could get a better look at his face and assess any hidden thoughts.

"I love you, Claire." He tightened his arms even more. "And I promise there will never be a next time as long as I have anything to say about it."

"Promises, promises," she joked, suddenly too uncertain to voice her own feelings until the arc from a nearby flashlight caught his face, and she saw unrestrained love in his eyes. "I love you too, Travis."

"I knew that."

"Did you now?" She mimicked his earlier comment.

A floodlight clicked on next to them just in time to glimpse the confidence fleeing from his face. "Let's say I hoped you did."

She couldn't bear his uncertainty. Had to fix it. Making sure her love burned as brightly as the floodlight, she peered deeply into his eyes. "I do. So much. Don't ever doubt it."

She laid her head on his chest and sighed in happiness. A sudden breeze kicked up, and despite his nearness, she shivered.

"Let's get you to the ambulance so we can leave this place." He stroked her cheek. "Can you walk?"

"I can, but..." She snuggled closer.

"Freeloader." He swung her up into his arms.

He held her firmly but tenderly as he moved at a rapid pace to the ambulance. He lowered her gently to the bumper and stepped back. Shoved his hands into his pockets. Moved again and rested a shoulder on the vehicle.

He was still worried. Uneasy. She hated that for him, but couldn't change it. The female medic with curly black hair disinfected and bound Claire's wrists, then checked her vitals. Travis's gaze remained fixed on the medic the entire time.

"You're good to go." The medic smiled and then climbed into her vehicle to stow her supplies.

Claire looked up at Travis and found that uncertainty still in his expression. She took his hand and twined their fingers together. He led her out of the spotlight.

She had to try to assure him of their future together. "I want you to know that I don't care how dangerous your job is. I won't send you away again. Ever."

He looked deeply into her eyes. "Is that why you broke things off with us?"

"After my dad...I was afraid something like that would happen to you too."

He tilted his head, still watching her. "Not that I'm not pleased, but why the sudden change of mind?"

"I get it now. After the last few days, I know I can't eliminate danger. You could be hurt in everyday things like driving a car." She ran her finger down the side of his face. "The only thing I ask is that we try to find a way to communicate in your long deployments."

"About that." He tightened his hold on her hand. "I was

thinking I'm ready for a more stable job. One where I'll be around for you and all the little Chapmans we might have."

Perfect. Or was it? "You can't do that for me. The Army needs you."

"And they'll have me. You know Colonel Lynch offered me a job at the institute. It's time for me to leave the team. To be stateside all the time so I can be with you."

She held Travis's gaze. "I suppose this means you'll have to kiss me to seal the deal."

"Oh, yeah." He grinned. "Now and copious times every day for the rest of our lives."

He swooped his head down. His lips claimed hers in a bruising kiss.

Claire heard strains of "What a Wonderful World" coming from the medic's phone, and she knew without a doubt every day would be wonderful now that her Green Beret was home for good.

20

Four weeks later.

Claire watched from above as waves crashed against the shore in the cove at Cold Harbor. Sharp and dangerous rock walls protruded below her. The sand at the water's edge a warm brown with frothy water lapping on the shore.

A beautiful setting. One Claire never imagined she would see, but here she was visiting Cold Harbor with Travis. He gripped her hand as if afraid she might take a tumble over the cliff.

So protective. She loved it.

She glanced over her shoulder at Gage. "Oregon beaches are so different from Florida beaches. Wind-swept, rugged, and uninhabited here. Buttery pristine sand, hot temperatures, and commercial establishments there."

Gage nodded. "They're nothing alike, and I prefer ours for sure."

"I think I do too." She took in the scenic view again.

"A lot of tourists would agree with you." He pointed to the left. "That island is one of our most popular locations to stay. It holds a small cabin—Heavenly Hideaway. It's only accessible by boat. Tourists from the big city flock to it for the privacy."

"Sounds, well...heavenly." She chuckled.

"It is." Gage's tone had deepened. "But it can be dangerous when a storm rolls in if the occupants don't stay buttoned down."

She imagined the wind kicking up on the ocean. The dark clouds. The water lashing up on the shore. Rain pelting down. Visibility zero. The small cabin shaking with the force of heavy rain. She shuddered.

"Cold?" Travis asked.

"No, just thinking how that island could change in a heartbeat."

"So true," Gage said. "Especially at this time of year when our rainy season sets in."

"Good thing we're staying with Gage then," Travis said. "How far away is your compound?"

"Sounds like you're itching to get there," Gage said.

"All the toys." Travis laughed.

"Then let's get moving," Gage said. "First, we can head down to the water, and Claire can get her feet wet." Gage pointed at their rental SUV behind them. Gage had offered to send a helicopter to pick them up in Portland, but they'd wanted to make the scenic drive, so they rented an SUV to make the long drive instead.

They crossed the viewing area and got in. They'd met up with Gage in the quaint little town, and he'd taken over driving to get them to his compound. He cranked the engine, and it roared to life, disturbing the calm only interrupted by seagulls and the rush of water. He wound them down the road that lazily followed the beach until they were driving onto the packed sand.

He parked near the advancing water. "Prepare yourself for cold water. It'll be in the fifties."

"That doesn't sound so cold." She grabbed her tote bag, holding a towel.

Gage killed the engine. "It's not for a short dip, but could still be deadly if you stayed in the water too long."

Travis leaned over the seat. "For reference, it takes at least thirty minutes in freezing water for hypothermia to set in for an average adult."

She hung her towel around her neck. "So capsizing in this water could be much more deadly than in Florida."

"Exactly," Gage said. "Something I hope everyone would take into account here. Doesn't happen. At least not by most tourists, and we have a lot of them."

Gage slid out of the vehicle and so did Claire. Travis followed. She kicked off her flip-flops and gasped at the cold sand underfoot. Gage was right. She was in for a surprise once she hit that water. She inched closer to the surf and let it tickle her toes. The biting cold had her jumping back.

"Wimp." Travis grabbed her hand and plowed them both into the surf.

She screamed and threw her arms around his neck, hoping he would lift her up out of the waves. He did, and she clung to him.

Gage's hearty laugh rolled through the air and disappeared in the chilly breeze. "Told you it was cold."

Travis carried her out to the solid but wet beach and set her down.

She looked at Gage. "I've learned my lesson. I will listen to you in the future."

"Mwahahaha." He rubbed his hands together. "Now you're ready to experience my compound according to my rules."

She and Travis laughed with him. It was hard to believe just a month ago she was in danger and these men were protecting her. Now she got to see the softer side of both guys and to witness the strong bond Travis shared with his buddy.

Travis had retired from the team as he'd said he would do and would start work in Orlando after they got back from this trip. They'd decided to take Gage up on his offer to visit him as a way to put an end to the terrible nightmare. She especially needed to let go of Julie's betrayal. The bloody tissue and Band-Aid wrapper matched back to her, cementing her guilt. Claire could hardly believe it, but the facts didn't lie.

And maybe let go of the betrayal by Mike, Warren, and Eric. They were in jail awaiting trial, as was Julie. The DA thought all four would be found guilty and serve max sentences for their crimes, and Claire now felt safe to go about her life again.

"Ready to go?" Gage asked. "You'll have plenty of time to come back this week."

"I wouldn't want to deprive Travis of seeing all your toys, so lead the way." She winked at Travis and jogged to the vehicle.

She sat on the side to brush off her feet and dry them, but Travis took her towel and knelt in front of her. He rubbed her feet until they were toasty warm and slipped her flip-flops on.

"Oh man," she said. "If this is the kind of treatment I get at the beach, we need to move here."

"This is vacation Travis," he said, humor in his tone. "Not work week Travis, so don't get used to it."

"Or plan a lot of vacations." She laughed and slid her legs into the vehicle. He closed the door and cleaned his own feet then climbed in the back.

Gage got them on the scenic road again. She looked up at the majestic evergreen trees and enjoyed seeing ferns bigger than she'd ever seen. Gage passed through the town with souvenir and antique stores, a bakery, other dining establishments, and a candy shop.

"I'll for sure be spending a morning exploring here." She looked over the seat at Travis. "Don't worry. You can stay at the compound and play with Gage's toys."

He flashed her a surprised look. "You know I'll come with you if you want me to."

She reached back and gave his hand a squeeze. "I appreciate that and love you all the more for your thoughtfulness."

Gage mocked gagging.

"Hey." She released Travis's hand. "Get used to it. You're going to see a lot of it this week."

Gage groaned, but Claire could see he was happy for them. She wished he could be happy again too. She'd seen moments of sadness when he didn't think anyone was watching. Claire couldn't be sure if it was due to the loss of his wife or the ongoing challenges his daughter faced with her brain injury. Either way, he was suffering, and she wanted everyone to experience the same joy that Travis had brought to her life in just a short time.

Gage turned off the road through a stand of tall evergreens that masked the drive so well that if you weren't looking for it, you would miss it. He pulled onto a secluded driveway, and a short way in, he stopped at a tall secured gate where a keypad was mounted on the post along with a camera and speaker. He lowered the window and tapped the keypad. The gate groaned open.

He pulled through, heading down a drive that led to an opening with a large house to the left and a driveway to the right.

He glanced in the rearview mirror. "Settle in or check out those toys?"

"Toys," Travis said. "I mean, if that's okay with you, Claire?"

"You could always go to the house and hang with my housekeeper and Mia if you don't want a tour," Gage said.

"I want to go wherever my sweetie goes," she said to get a response from Gage.

He rolled his eyes and laughed. "You're right. It's gonna be a long, painful week."

He turned down the drive to the right. "Ahead, you'll see the staff cabins and cabins for guests who sign up for our training workshops."

Down the road sat five cabins, all a different design, each one unique. "I assume the personalized cabins are for staff."

Gage nodded. "Each person designed and built their place. You can tell a lot about them by the structure they built."

One was a traditional log cabin. One super modern. One A-frame. One a stark, no-frills cabin. The last a contemporary square box. She hoped after she got to know all of them this week that she could pin the cabin to the person.

"The plain log cabins are for the trainees." Gage pointed at a large barn-like building opposite the line of simple log cabins. "On the left is our training facility and weapons lock up. We'll come back to that after we tour the rest."

"Looks like a first-rate place you got here." Travis's tone held his ongoing excitement.

"We try." Gage may have downplayed the compliment, but he stuck out his chest as he drove past the training facility. Further down the road, he approached a treelined town with building facades lining the paved street. They included a bank, post office, grocery store, and other retail stores. It even had a Starbucks.

"We use this street for our urban tactical drills," Gage

said. "I patterned it after the FBI's Hogan's Alley but on a much smaller scale."

"Impressive." Travis leaned forward. "I hope you'll include me in one of your drills. Or two or three or all of them while I'm here."

"You got it. You can show the participants what not to do when under siege." Gage laughed and glanced at Claire. "Don't worry. We don't use live ammo."

"I would hope not."

He drove into a clearing holding a small hangar and helipad where a large helicopter was tied down to the pad. Claire knew nothing about choppers, but this was a pretty blue and white number sparkling clean under the soft sun filtering through the trees.

Travis let out a low whistle. "She's a beaut."

"I know, right?" Gage grinned and parked the vehicle. "Coop heads up air assault classes, and in the distance is our firing range."

"I'm sorry, honey." Travis reached for her hand. "I'm about to totally ignore you, and I apologize in advance."

"It's okay," she said. "As long as it doesn't become a habit."

He frowned. "No habit, but I suspect there will be more times this week than you would like."

She smiled at him. "I'm good with that. Go. Enjoy yourself."

He dropped her hand and bolted out of the vehicle. She took her time getting out, listening to Gage describe his helicopter and its versatility in hauling people and cargo. She'd had no idea his operation was so grand and that they faced dangerous situations such as kidnapping.

Travis took it all in, his eyes filled with longing. Intense and unyielding. Had he made the right decision to leave his team?

Her stomach twisted into a hard knot.

Would he come to regret his decision? Resent her?

If so, how would she handle such emotion coming from the man she wanted to spend the rest of her life with, and could their relationship survive?

⁓

Travis needed to get Claire alone for a few minutes before meeting up with the team in the training room. So he'd sent Gage ahead with the SUV, and Travis walked with her toward the facility, giving them an even closer look at the small town.

Wow, Gage had it all. Top-notch operation all the way. Not a surprise. Gage was a top-notch kind of guy.

Travis suspected he was still drooling over the helo. A pricey number for sure. Travis didn't want to experience a life-altering injury, but he wouldn't mind working on a team like Gage's. Or maybe once Claire finished her project, he could even start his own team.

The odd look on her face said she wouldn't like that idea. Not at all. But she'd said she was good with him staying on the team, and a tactical group like Gage's was less dangerous than military ops. He would only consider it if Claire agreed. She was top priority in his life right now, and he would never do anything to upset that.

At least he hoped he wasn't about to upset it.

He stopped in front of the picturesque chapel at the edge of Gage's fake town. A rustic bench sat out front of the small white building, and he urged Claire to sit.

She peered at him. "But Gage and the team are waiting for us."

"They can wait a few minutes. I want to ask you something." He got down on his knee and pulled out the ring box he'd tucked into his pocket.

She gasped. "Is this...?"

"Yes," he said, trying to see through her shocked reaction to the happiness he hoped to find.

She fanned her face.

"This might seem sudden since we've only been back together for a month, but I've had this ring for years. I was going to propose when you asked me to leave."

She grabbed his free hand. "I'm so, so sorry I did that. I ruined everything."

"No. You gave us a chance to be certain of what we want. I figure if we want the same thing twice it has to be right."

She gave a sharp nod. "I agree."

"And if you hadn't been afraid back then, would you have said yes to me?"

"Yes."

"And now? I love you, Claire. Everything about you. Your kindness. Loyalty. Inquisitive nature. Dedication to making the world a better place. Even your stubbornness."

"Really?" She batted her lashes at him. "The stubbornness?"

He nodded.

Her lips tipped in a slight smile. "I'll probably have to remind you of that over the years."

"Then does that mean you'll marry me?" he asked, needing to hear her officially answer him.

"I will. I do. Yes." She threw her arms around his neck before he could get the ring out and hugged him tight. "I love you too, Travis. For many of the same reasons, but I'll also add your willingness to retire for me."

"About that." He leaned back and shared his recent thoughts about the future.

"I'd be open to that for sure. Sounds like a way to do what you love in a safer environment."

His joy needed a release. He scooped her off the bench and into his arms, stood, and swung her around.

She giggled like a little girl, and he set her down.

She gave him a pointed look. "Now, about that ring."

"I hope I did all right. I got a black diamond. They symbolize power, passion, and inner strength. The way I think of you. And I just plain thought it was unique—like you are."

The suspense of waiting for her reaction was far worse than the suspense on any op that had taken a wrong turn, so he quickly flipped open the box to display the hexagonal-cut black diamond with smaller white diamonds on a thin band.

She gazed at it, her mouth opening and closing and opening again. She met his gaze. "Oh, Travis. It's beautiful. And unique, like you said. I love it."

He let out his breath and slid the ring onto her finger. It fit perfectly, and his body welled with emotion. She held out her hand, admiring the ring as she twisted and turned it in the sunlight. The diamonds glinted.

She looked up. "I don't want a long engagement. I want a simple wedding as soon as possible."

"Probably not at this place." He glanced at the chapel. "Would be hard for our guests since there's no inside seating."

She grinned. "So you agree? The sooner the better?"

He drew her into his arms and kissed her neck. "Soon. Real soon. But at least let me get a look at that weapons' room first."

She tossed back her head and laughed. "Life with you, Travis Chapman, is going to be very interesting."

"And I suspect trying at times." He paused for a breath.

"But for every misstep I take, I promise to make it up to you in the most interesting ways."

"Ooh, then, Travis." She cocked her head and studied him. "Start misbehaving so I can see the lengths of your creativity."

He laughed and hugged her tight. How he hadn't gone back to Orlando to fight for this amazing woman when she'd sent him away the first time was beyond him. But it was a certainty that he wasn't going to do anything on purpose to call their relationship into question again. He would have that sappy vision he'd imagined with her. Sunshiny mornings. Little children running around. Cookies in the kitchen.

And if none of that ever happened after they got married, he would never tire of coming home to a woman who tested him in the best of ways and made him a better person. The person he and God wanted him to be.

The COLD HARBOR SERIES

Meet Blackwell Tactical- former military and law enforcement heroes who will give everything to protect innocents... even their own lives.

For More Details Visit -
www.susansleeman.com/books/cold-harbor/

THE TRUTH SEEKERS
People are rarely who they seem

A twin who didn't know she had a sister. A mother whose child isn't her own. A woman whose parents lied to her. All needing help from The Truth Seekers forensic team.

Book 1 - Dead Ringer
Book 2 - Dead Silence
Book 3 - Dead End
Book 4 - Dead Heat
Book 5 - Dead Center
Book 6 - Dead Even

For More Details Visit -
www.susansleeman.com/books/truth-seekers/

NIGHTHAWK SECURITY SERIES
Protecting others when unspeakable danger lurks.

A woman being stalked. A mother and child being hunted. And more. All in danger. Needing protection from the men of Nighthawk Security.

Book 1 – Night Fall
Book 2 – Night Vision
Book 3 – Night Hawk
Book 4 – Night Moves
Book 5 – Night Watch
Book 6 – Night Prey

For More Details Visit -
www.susansleeman.com/books/nighthawk-security/

STEELE GUARDIAN SERIES
Intrigue. Suspense. Family.

A kidnapped baby. A jewelry heist. Amnesia. Abduction. Smuggled antiquities. And in every book, God's amazing power and love.

Book 1 – Tough as Steele
Book 2 – Nerves of Steele
Book 3 – Forged in Steele
Book 4 – Made of Steele
Book 5 – Solid as Steele
Book 6 – Edge of Steele

For More Details Visit -
www.susansleeman.com/books/steele-guardians

SHADOW LAKE SURVIVAL SERIES

When survival takes a dangerous turn and lives are on the line.

The men of Shadow Lake Survival impart survival skills and keep those in danger safe from harm. Even if it means risking their lives.

Book 1 – Shadow of Deceit
Book 2 – Shadow of Night
Book 3 – Shadow of Truth
Book 4 – Shadow of Hope – April 8, 2024
Book 5 – Shadow of Doubt – July 8, 2024
Book 6 – Shadow of Fear – November 4, 2024

For More Details Visit -
www.susansleeman.com/books/shadow-lake-survival

ABOUT SUSAN

SUSAN SLEEMAN is a bestselling and award-winning author of more than 50 inspirational/Christian and clean read romantic suspense books. In addition to writing, Susan also hosts the website, TheSuspenseZone.com.

Susan currently lives in Oregon, but has had the pleasure of living in nine states. Her husband is a retired church music director and they have two beautiful daughters, two very special sons-in-law, and three amazing grandsons.

For more information visit:
www.susansleeman.com

Made in the USA
Middletown, DE
13 February 2024